"The perfect cure for a lover's exhaustion..."

Janet held a chocolate chip cookie out to Eric, then laughed as he bit into it ferociously.

"These are good, even if I did make them myself," he murmured, smacking his lips. "But I spy a few errant crumbs...." Bending over, he touched his tongue to the swell of her breasts. Warming to his task, he found another crumb, then nudged the blanket aside, searching for more. "We have to be careful they don't wind up in the sheets."

"I agree," Janet breathed, luxuriating in the caresses spreading over her like sunshine. His moist kisses trailed to her navel, and she moaned with desire. "But I don't think baking is your finest talent...."

THE AUTHOR

Never let it be said that romance writers aren't sticklers for accuracy. To get the comic protest scene just right for this Temptation, Georgia Bockoven went to a maximum-security research lab—and came close to being arrested for poking around. Fortunately her fast talking saved the day—and the scene. Georgia's writing for both Temptation and Superromance is notable for its timeliness and warmth.

Recent Books by Georgia Bockoven

A Week from Friday

GEORGIA BOCKOVEN

Harlequin Books

TORONTO • NEW YORK • LONDON
AMSTERDAM • PARIS • SYDNEY • HAMBURG
STOCKHOLM • ATHENS • TOKYO • MILAN

This one's for Mary Gulden,
one of those rare people who
made everyone she met feel special.

———————————————————

Published February 1986

ISBN 0-373-25194-7

1

"YOU WANT ME to do *what*?" Janet Franklin twisted sideways in an effort to move faster down the crowded hallway. Her friend, Casey Ellington, hurried after her, clutching an armful of books to her chest.

"Please, Janet!" Casey wailed. "I've been working on this guy for months."

"Why can't you go out with him tomorrow night? Then you could steal the car yourself tonight." Out of the corner of her eye, Janet saw an indignant look flash across Casey's round face as her four-foot-eleven-inch friend bulldozed her way through the crowd that had started to separate them.

"I don't steal cars," Casey hissed, coming up to Janet's elbow. "I repossess them. There's a big difference."

"To you, maybe, but I doubt that's how the guys who think they own the cars feel."

Casey sighed dramatically. "And here I thought you would jump at the chance to make two hundred dollars."

Janet pulled Casey over to the wall to get out of the flowing crush of people. Her eyes narrowed. "*Two hundred dollars?* For repossessing one car?" That was enough money to pay for next semester's books with a little left over. When Casey nodded, Janet felt herself weakening. "Tell me what I would have to do."

"Thanks, Janet. I knew you wouldn't let me down."

"Wait a minute, I haven't said I'd do it yet." But Casey ignored her disclaimer.

"Meet me in the cafeteria at the student union after class, and I'll fill you in on all the details." Before Janet could say anything more, Casey started back the way she had come, quickly disappearing into the crowd.

Janet gazed down the hallway a few seconds longer before climbing the stairs to her biology class. As usual, she was the last to arrive. She threaded her way through the room to her table and gave her lab partner, Earthquake, a thankful smile for getting there early enough to set up the equipment they would be using that day. While a little on the strange side, with his Mohawk haircut and a message for the day written on either side of his shaved scalp, Earthquake had a brilliant scientific mind and was a godsend to Janet, who had only marginal talent for science and, moreover, invariably gagged through every dissection.

Two years ago, Earthquake had come west to Stanford from an exclusive New England prep school. His transformation from preppy to punk had occurred shortly after his arrival in California—much to the consternation of his straight-arrow parents. His colorful name—which his parents steadfastly refused to acknowledge—had been adopted in celebration of his new life-style.

Despite the years and social mores that separated them, Janet and Earthquake had developed a friendship that was based on a genuine liking for each other. She patiently tolerated his jabs about her being twenty-seven and—when she struggled with a new concept—about her being handicapped by mental infirmities, and he begrudgingly put up with her smugness when she consistently scored higher on tests than he did.

Sitting down on the next stool, she slipped her books underneath the table and reached into her purse to pull out a rubber band. With a few deft movements, she quickly had her shoulder-length black hair gathered into a ponytail and out of her way. Her blue eyes sparkling mischievously, she turned to Earthquake and took his chin in her hand. "Turn sideways," she commanded. "I want to read today's pithy pronouncement. I need an omen to tell me what to do about a job I'm considering."

He dutifully turned his head. "Sorry," he said with an air of disdain. "Today's message is for dreamers. If you want your tea leaves read, check the cafeteria. There may be someone lurking around who can help you." For the first time she noticed that he had dyed his normally platinum stripe of hair to look like a rainbow. Above his ear, in black ink, he had written, Somewhere Over, with an arrow pointing up.

Janet grimaced as she shook her head. "Not one of your better efforts." She studied his hair, bending forward to get a closer look. "How did you get all those colors on there so evenly?"

"Trade secret."

She laughed. "Oh? And whose trade might that be?"

"Get with it, Janet." He reached over to give her ponytail a playful tug. "Even Macy's has a punk department nowadays."

"First Macy's and then the world? Is that the plan?"

His indignant answer was cut off in midsentence when the professor entered the room.

JANET TOOK POSSESSION of the last empty table in the cafeteria, scattering her books across the top and placing her hand peremptorily on the single extra chair. She glanced at her watch—eleven forty-five. She had less than an hour to go to the library and to drive home. If Casey didn't come soon, she was going to have to repossess the car herself.

"*There* you are."

Janet swung around to see her friend coming toward her, carrying a trayful of food. She frowned. "Casey, I can't—"

"It's my treat."

"That wasn't what I was going to say...." But it could have been. Janet's tight budget was common knowledge among her friends. She had never tried, or seen any reason, to pretend that things were any better financially than they were. Even with a major portion of her tuition covered by grants and with the rest paid for by loans, supporting herself and an ancient Volkswagen required an incredible ongoing monetary juggling routine.

"I know, I know...you have to be home by one o'clock so you can baby-sit Carol's kid. That still gives you time enough to eat something."

"But—"

"But nothing. You eat; I'll talk." Casey purposely eyed Janet, covering her from head to toe with a sweeping glance. "Even with all those clothes on, I can tell you've lost weight again. It's elegant to be tall and thin, Jan, but your bones shouldn't rattle when you walk."

"Thanks a lot. How am I supposed to feel after this pep talk? Up? Down? Encouraged that I have a friend who cares…or depressed because I'm not long for this world?"

"It was just a casual observation; don't get in a huff." She took a salad, a sandwich and milk off the tray and handed them to Janet.

"We have to make this fast, Casey. I told Carol I would try to get home a little early today." She opened the milk and stuck in a straw. "First tell me something about this outfit you're working for. Then we'll get on to whether I'm actually going to steal that car for you tonight."

Shaking her head, Casey let out a long sigh. "You're sure making a big deal out of a simple favor." When it became obvious Janet was not going to ease off on her demands, Casey went on. "Louie is a subcontractor to over half of the banks in San Francisco—which means that whenever someone defaults on a car loan, the banks call Louie. For years he handled all the work himself, but when the economy took a downturn and half the world stopped paying on their loans, he had to hire help. He prefers using women for repossessions because he thinks they aren't as likely as a man to arouse suspicion if they fumble around a little trying to get into a car."

Janet swallowed a bite of her ham and cheese sandwich. "I don't know about this, Casey. It sounds dangerous. What happens if the guy who owns the car catches you?"

"That's the best part about working for Louie. He studies the habits of the owners before he ever sends anyone out. For instance, the car you're to take tonight belongs to a guy who goes jogging around the Presidio three times a week. All you have to do is be there when he takes off, and you have at least half an hour to work."

"How—"

"With these." She pulled a ring of keys from her purse.

Janet's eyes widened. "There must be a hundred keys—"

"It's not as bad as it looks. I've never had to go through more than twenty before I found the right one."

"Okay, let's say I get the car. What then?"

"You drive to the corner of Market and Second Street; Louie takes it from there. You can catch either a bus or a cab back to your own car and head home two hundred dollars richer."

It sounded easy. So why the strange feeling in the pit of her stomach? "Casey, are you absolutely sure this is on the up and up?"

Her friend looked wounded. "Do you think I would be involved in anything that wasn't?"

"You've done some crazy things—"

"*I've done crazy things?* You throw pretty big rocks for someone who lives in such a great big glass house. When was the last time you saw *me* dressed up like a gorilla . . . or a chicken? Have I ever caught pneumonia standing around in a fog wearing a skimpy swimming suit, trying to pass out hors d'oeuvres to yachtsmen who had sense enough to stay home? Have you ever—"

"That's enough . . . you've made your point." A year and a half earlier, Janet's ongoing effort to make ends meet had led her to the Anything Goes Agency. It was an ideal job for someone in her position—flexible hours, good pay and terrific tips. Granted, she had done some strange things to earn her money—everything from dressing up as a clown and delivering balloons to a man painting the Golden Gate Bridge, to demonstrating a "revolutionary" new vegetable peeler at a trade show in the Cow Palace. But working for the agency was ideally suited to her needs, as was the limousine chauffeuring job. She still held both jobs.

Casey sat back in her chair, a triumphant smile reaching her large brown eyes and making them dance. "You'll do the job, right?"

"I suppose...." The money was just too good to pass up. She'd deal with the lingering doubts later.

"I owe you one, Jan. This could be the most important date of my life—I think I'm falling in love."

Janet mentally groaned as she looked at her beaming friend. Casey was forever falling in love. She took the napkin from her lap, folded it and put it back on the tray. Could she ever have been that young and naive? Of course she had. Why else would she be where she was now—divorced, broke and, at twenty-seven years old, only a sophomore in college?

By THE TIME Janet reached the Presido at six-thirty that night, a dense fog had worked its way into the old parklike military base. She was early, having planned for a rush hour traffic jam that never occurred. Beyond her field of vision, she heard the sounds of the last of the commuter's cars as they headed for the Golden Gate Bridge and home. The freeway and a few hundred yards of shoreline were all that separated the parking lot where she waited from San Francisco Bay. Behind her, on the shoreline, were pine and eucalyptus trees and rolling grasslands.

Unlike most military bases, the fifteen-hundred-acre Presidio was open to civilian traffic. Founded the year the colonies declared independence from England, the base was now more important historically than functionally.

Janet had always loved coming to this incongruously peaceful place of forest and wildlife nestled within California's second largest city. She didn't mind waiting. It had been so long since she'd spent any time at the Presidio that she found she was actually looking forward to the quarter-mile walk to the lower parking lot, where she was to wait for the navy-blue Shelby Cobra to arrive. Because she hadn't any idea what a Cobra looked like, she had stopped by the library to peruse several classic-car magazines. After studying a few of the pictures, she decided she didn't much care for the low-slung two-seater. If the choice had been hers, she would have spent the money on a new Mercedes sports car.

After another self-indulgent ten minutes, which she spent absorbing the beauty of her muted surroundings and remembering the bicycle trips she had made through the area with Robert when they were married, she reached for the book lying on the bucket seat beside her. Sometime before seven-thirty the next morning, she had to read *Measure for Measure* and prepare herself to intelligently discuss the double entendres Shakespeare had used throughout the play. Stifling a yawn, she opened the book.

It soon became obvious that she would get little studying done. Between glancing at her watch and then lingeringly at the fog-shrouded woods, she had read less than five pages in fifteen minutes. Snapping the book shut with a satisfying thud, she opened the Volkswagen's creaking door and stepped outside. How marvelous the air smelled—the distinctive eucalyptus mixed with the sea and with a touch of pine and moist earth.

But the mist was cold, and she was soon hugging herself to ward off the chill. Hoping to appear inconspicuous, she had worn a gray utilitarian sweat suit, and it was suddenly feeling like a skimpy layer of nylon. She pulled the hood up and tied the strings so that it fit snugly around her face before she took off over the hill.

Tall wet grass brushed against her legs and cushioned her footsteps as she passed through the swirling mists. To make sure the Cobra's owner didn't spot her watching him, she had originally planned to do her observing at a safe distance from the parking lot. But the fog had grown so thick that she was forced to find a hiding place behind a pine tree that was less than ten yards from where she'd been told he always parked his car.

She didn't have long to wait. Twin tunnels of light swung around the curve and moved in her direction. Her heart lurched when the light caught and reflected off the minute particles of water suspended around her, and she flattened herself against the pine and felt its rough bark dig into her cheek.

What was she doing here? If she wasn't the sneak thief she tried to tell herself she wasn't, then why did she feel like one? She took several deep calming breaths, reminding herself as she did so that what she was doing was not only legal, it was moral. If someone would not willingly return what no longer belonged to them, then it was certainly proper to see that the rightful owner regained possession.

What a load of horse manure. What if the poor guy had been stricken with a debilitating disease that had made him lose his job, and his car was his only means of transportation to and from the doctor? Or what if he had lost everything else he owned when the law office he had set up in a ghetto went under? What if— The lights went out. Slowly she moved her head until one eye peeked around the tree trunk. When she saw her intended victim in the dim light of the street lamp, she caught her lip between her teeth.

He was so big. If something went wrong and he caught her trying to steal his car, she wouldn't stand a chance. She thought about the simple karate moves Earthquake had insisted on teaching her last month before they had gone into a seedy neighborhood to pass out antinuclear pamphlets. She rolled her eyes in disgust. The moves just might work all right—if she could get her attacker to stand perfectly still while she set up the takedown. Then again, if he should decide not to cooperate, there was always the chance that he might counter her efforts with a carefully thought-out flick of his wrist and send her sailing across the bay to Oakland.

The man walked past the front of the car and put his foot on a wooden railing to begin a series of stretching exercises. Janet tried to make herself smaller. He was so close that she could almost touch him. She knew it was insanity to continue watching, yet she couldn't stop. A spider observing a hornet flying toward its web might feel as she did—frightened, yet mesmerized by the possibilities of the encounter.

Suddenly he straightened and looked around. Janet sucked in her breath. For the briefest instant their eyes met; she saw intelligence and wit in the dark depths of his as he returned her gaze. Her heart pounded loudly in her ears while she waited for him to call out to her, demanding to know why she was spying on him. But there was only silence. She must have imagined something had passed between them.

After several seconds his forehead wrinkled in a frown, and he rubbed the back of his neck before glancing around again. He walked back to the car, dug his keys out of the inside pocket of his sweat suit, locked the door and took off at an easy, loping jog.

Janet stepped around the tree to watch him leave. His stride appeared slightly off balance, as if one of his shoes were a size too small or he had a cramp in his leg. As soon as the dense fog absorbed him, she moved over to the car. Her hands trembled as she held the large ring of keys in front of her. Arbitrarily she chose one to begin with. It took three tries to connect the chosen key to the keyhole and two jabs to realize it wasn't going to go in no matter how hard she pushed.

She looked down at the silver-colored key she held clamped between her finger and thumb, and the enormity of what she was about to do struck her anew. *Was she out of her mind?* What had ever induced her to agree to do something so stupid? With growing panic she tried the next key. Now that she was actually in the process of stealing the Incredible Hulk's car, the two hundred dollars no longer seemed such a gigantic amount. She went on to the next key. Never again, she vowed. If Casey should ever so much as hint that she wanted her to steal another car, she was going to run for the nearest exit. A self-deprecatory smile twitched at the corners of her mouth. Who was she trying to kid? All Casey would have to do would be to catch her at the end of the month, when two hundred dollars sounded like two thousand, and she would steal a Mack truck.

ERIC STEWART tried to ignore the threatening cramp in his thigh as he gradually increased his running pace. He couldn't believe how out of shape six weeks in a leg cast had left him or—even three weeks since the cast had been removed—how hard it still was to get back into the groove of regular exercise. Running wasn't something he did for its much-touted "high," or because he was "into" anything; it was simply something he did to counter the eight to ten hours he spent behind a desk every day. The accident that had put his leg in the cast, and his car in the shop, had also reinforced his conviction that life was too short not to live it to the fullest. And if that meant running to keep in shape, so be it—boring or not.

His thoughts digressed from his still-stiff leg to the phone call he had made to Hong Kong. He had wanted to tell his vacationing parents about the accident before they heard about it from his sister. He chuckled at the memory. Once his father had ascertained that Eric was going to live, he had skipped the minor details of his son's injuries and gone straight to asking about the damage done to the car. It wasn't until Eric had detailed every scratch and dint, and had convinced his father that they were only minor that he got him to calm down. Will Stewart was a rational man about anything and everything save two things—his family and the Shelby Cobra he had ceremoniously passed on to his only son the day Eric became a full partner in San Francisco's leading corporate law firm.

Eric had been so overwhelmed by the gift that he had been speechless. Until the day Will gave Eric the car, he and Susan had jokingly speculated on the arrangements their father had made to take the Cobra with him when he died. But all Eric's condescending thoughts had abruptly changed when he took ownership. Within days, he began to understand his father's intense pride in such a magnificent machine. The Cobra did everything a car was supposed to do and did it better than any other vehicle on the road. At least that was Eric's and Will's unshakable opinion. As far as they were concerned, anyone who didn't agree was either pathetically uninformed or incredibly pigheaded.

After Eric had owned the car a while, it turned out that the only major difference between father and son as far as love for the Cobra was their philosophy on how best to appreciate it. When Will had owned the Cobra he had locked it in a temperature-controlled garage, to be dusted and admired and never taken out except for a drive around the block or to be trailered to car shows. Eric took every bit as much care—fanatically listening and responding to every nuance of the motor and chassis—only he drove the car daily, using it for transportation to and from work.

Lost in his musings, Eric completed the second curve in his looping course. Suddenly a sound drifted through the fog that made his heart catch in his throat. It was a sound he recognized as clearly as his own voice—the throaty roar of the Cobra's engine. His one nightmare was coming true—*someone was stealing his car*.

Dammit! A frustrated groan passed his lips. He felt completely helpless. He had heard enough about car thieves and how they operated to know that once a car like the Cobra was gone, it was gone forever. It would be cut up for parts or shipped across the country within days. If he was going to do something, he had to do it fast.

Adrenaline surged through him. He searched through the fog for a familiar landmark, trying to decide whether it was shorter to go on or head back the way he had come. He made his choice and sprinted forward.

He arrived at the top of the hill overlooking the parking lot just in time to see the Cobra's headlights swing around the corner and out onto the main street. Saying a silent prayer that the thief would take another hard left onto the back road to avoid traffic, he started down the other side of the hill and headed toward the narrow road that led out of the Presidio.

Because he had less than half the distance to cover to get to the road and because Janet couldn't get the Cobra out of first gear and was therefore going less than twenty miles an hour, Eric arrived first. Mentally calculating how fast the Cobra was coming and how much time he needed to get out of the way if his plan didn't work, Eric stepped in front of the moving car, waving his hands.

Janet was frantically trying to get the Cobra into second gear, and she didn't look up until she was almost on top of Eric. She let out a terrified scream. With the fog swirling around him and the glare of the headlights bleaching his coloring, he filled the roadway in front of her like a gigantic apparition. By reflex, she jerked the steering wheel to the right. After that everything seemed to happen at once. The car skidded sideways, lurched and plummeted down an embankment. When it finally stopped going forward, it started to roll over onto its left side. For several breathtaking seconds it teetered on two wheels, then with a creaking groan, slowly righted itself. In front of her, the headlights stabbed the milky blackness ineffectually, as if she had landed in a void.

Janet sat very still, listening to the silence, waiting for her body to tell her whether she should try to move. When nothing cried out in pain, she tentatively eased herself upright in the driver's seat. So far, so good. She flexed her toes, rotated her ankles and bent her elbows. Everything seemed to be working as usual. She reached for the handle; it moved freely, but the door wouldn't open. She tried again, only this time, she used her shoulder to give it a little push. Nothing. She braced herself to exert more pressure, then the sound of something crashing through the bushes behind her made her decide it might be wiser for her to stay where she was. It was probably an illusion, but she felt there was a modicum of safety in her steel-and-glass cocoon.

As Eric started down the ravine, he hit his stiff leg against a tree stump. When he bent over to clasp his throbbing thigh, he lost his balance and rolled down the hill. He landed on his side, and looked up to realize he had stopped directly beside the Cobra. He instantly forgot about himself and began looking for signs of damage to the car. But reflecting off the fog, the headlights provided only enough light to let him see that the thief was still inside. He struggled to his feet, blind fury guiding his actions. Standing beside the softly hissing vehicle, his voice filled with menace, he glared at the figure behind the steering wheel. "Get out...."

Janet looked through the window and into the angriest eyes she had ever seen. She inched away from the door. "I can't...." She had meant to sound confident, but her words had come out as little more than a pathetic squeak. "It's stuck," she added, the words equally high-pitched.

Eric bent over to peer into the car. His eyes widened in surprise. A *woman* had stolen his car. He continued to stare at her, studying her in the soft light coming from the dashboard. She didn't look like a car thief. But then again, what was a car thief supposed to look like? He tried to open the door himself. He was no more successful than she had been. Thinking he might be able to work the handle from the inside, he demanded, "Roll down the window."

"Hah!" Not even the three little pigs had been that stupid. It didn't take a genius to figure out that the hands clenching and unclenching at his sides were doing so because they were anxious to get around her neck.

Closing his eyes, Eric took a deep breath and told himself to calm down. It didn't work. His fury had a mind of its own. "Look," he said in a deadly monotone, "either you roll down the window, or you can get out of the way while I break it in." This was pure bluff, but it sounded good. He was as incapable of purposely smashing one of the Cobra's windows as he was of passing by a Salvation Army kettle at Christmas without emptying his pockets of change.

It was more his tone of voice than the threatening words that convinced Janet that she wasn't dealing with a rational man. She decided to stall for time, hoping someone had seen the car go over the embankment and had called for help. "I'll open the window if, and when, you calm down—and not before." She sounded like a mother chastising her child.

Eric leaned his arms on the side of the car at the base of the window and pressed his face close to the glass. "Since that's not likely to happen any time before next week, I'd suggest you do what I ask before I get any angrier."

So much for defiance. Maybe reasoning would work. "What are you so mad about, anyway? You must have known this was going to happen sooner or later. After all, banks have never been known for their warmheartedness. Try to look on the bright side. You probably won't even have to pay the insurance deductible to have this thing fixed; the bank will be liable for it."

He stared at her. "Would you mind running that by me one more time?"

At least he was talking to her in a more normal tone of voice. "If you had kept up your payments," she went on, "none of this would have happened. Actually, in a way, this whole thing tonight is all your fault."

"Payments?" he repeated. "My fault?"

She was on a roll. "What's more, because of your irresponsible behavior, I'm undoubtedly out the two hundred dollars I was supposed to be paid for this job. And on top of everything else, I'll probably flunk my English Lit test tomorrow because I'll never get home in time to study for it tonight."

This time it was Eric's turn to back away. Either the beautiful young woman sitting on the other side of the window had hit her head in the crash, or he was dealing with someone playing with a woefully short deck. He held his hands out in a gesture of goodwill. "See...I've calmed down. Now do you think you might roll down the window for me?"

She eyed him suspiciously. "Why are you talking to me like that?"

"Like what?" He forced a smile.

"Like you're dealing with a two-year-old." Somehow she had trusted him more when he was yelling at her. Suddenly the air above him took on a pulsating red glow. Janet's gaze moved to the top of the hill; Eric's followed. As they stared, a disembodied, mechanically aided voice shattered the stillness. "Are you all right down there?"

In response to the intrusion, both Janet and Eric let out private sighs of relief. "Thank God," they simultaneously murmured.

2

A SPOTLIGHT swept back and forth across the ravine before coming to rest on the wrecked car and its occupant. Within minutes two policemen were climbing down the hillside and heading toward them. Janet decided she had never been so relieved to see anyone. They weren't riding white horses or sounding a bugle call, but that didn't stop her from feeling as though she were a trapped settler with the cavalry coming to the rescue.

When the policemen arrived, the first thing they did was ask Janet if she was hurt; the next, after they had tried opening her door, was to go around and open the passenger door. As she got out, she and Eric exchanged sheepish glances. Neither of them had thought to do anything so logical.

The younger of the two officers asked for Eric's identification. While he took down the information, the older one turned to Janet. He eyed her coolly, but as far as she could tell, unjudgmentally. "Now, then, why don't you tell me what's going on here?"

Where should she start? The past two days had begun to take on the wacky nature of a French farce. She took a deep breath and decided it was best to begin at the beginning. "My name is Janet Franklin. I want you to know that I don't usually do this kind of work.... That's probably why I've made such a mess of things tonight. I'm only here because my friend, Casey El-lington, thinks she's in love again. You see, she had this hot date for this evening, and insisted she would die if she couldn't keep it, so I said I would take over for her—"

The officer lowered the pencil he had held poised over his notebook and looked at her with narrowed eyes. "Why don't you skip over the motivations for the time being and simply tell me how you came to be in this man's car at the bottom of this gully."

She gave him a quick grin. "Just the facts, huh?"

He nodded.

"Well, I'll do my best. Casey works for this man named Louie who—"

"What's Louie's last name?"

Janet thought a moment, then shook her head. She was sure she had never heard Casey mention Louie's last name.

"It may come to you."

"I don't think so. Casey said his name several times, but I'm sure she never used anything other than Louie."

"We'll work on it later. For now, why don't you just go on with the story."

She was fairly sure he didn't want to hear about the state of the economy or about how people were miss-ing loan payments, so she skipped over that part. "Louie has this business repossessing cars for banks when they have someone who is delinquent on their loan. This past year the workload became so heavy that he had to hire help. Casey is one of his employees. . . ." She suddenly realized the other officer had stopped talking and was watching her, his eyes lighted with a knowing smile.

"Go on," the older policeman prodded.

She felt a peculiar lump in her throat. "And as I told you before, Casey asked me to help her out tonight, so I did."

"Let me be sure I've got this straight. You were in the process of repossessing this car when you had the accident, is that right?"

The lump was growing. "Uh-huh."

The policeman turned to Eric. "And what do you have to say about all of this?"

"This car has been in my family for twenty years. Not once, in all that time, has there ever been a loan against it."

Janet tried to swallow. "He's lying," she managed to say. "He has to be," she added in a choked whisper.

"Can I see the registration?" the older policeman asked.

Eric went around the car, opened the glove box and took out a piece of paper. He handed it to the officer. After he had checked the registration, he turned it so that Janet could see. "There's only one name listed, ma'am, just Mr. Stewart's—not any bank."

"There has to be a mistake."

"Yes," he said slowly. "I'd say that's probably true. Now if you'll just come along with me, I'm sure we can find out more about this 'mistake' down at the station."

"'Station?' You want me to go to a police station?"

"If you don't mind," he said, his voice dripping sarcasm.

As Eric watched Janet, he was surprised to discover he believed her crazy story. At least, he believed *she* believed what she said. He doubted anyone could fake the transformation he had just witnessed. Her arrogant confidence had disappeared, leaving her as wide-eyed and terrified looking as a wild animal caught in a trap.

They went over to the embankment and began climbing up the slick surface. Halfway to the top, Janet lost her footing and let out a gasp as she started to slide backward. Eric braced himself and reached out to catch her.

"Thanks," she said, brushing debris from her sweat pants.

He stared down at her. "Purely reflex, I assure you."

She glanced up to see if he was serious. Large dark noncommittal eyes stared back into hers. "Listen . . . I'm truly sorry about your car. I'll pay for the damages." Just how she would go about paying him she hadn't worked out yet.

Slowly the menacing snarl became a lopsided grin. "I'd like to be there when you explain this to your insurance agent."

"Oh, I doubt that I'll go through the insurance company. I can't afford to have them raise my rates again."

He ignored the "again." "And you think it would be cheaper to pay for the repairs yourself?" He thought of the bill he had recently paid for the "minor" bodywork performed on the Cobra. It had been only a few hundred dollars less than a first-year law clerk's annual salary.

"I have a friend who does this kind of repair work on the side. He's not only reasonable, he'll let me pay the bill a little at a time." When Eric didn't immediately answer, she added, "Don't worry, he does beautiful work. I ran into a concrete pole with my Volkswagen last summer and almost wiped out the entire front end. When Phil was through with the car, it looked as good as new."

A flashlight beam swept over them. "I think our escorts are beginning to wonder what's keeping us." Eric reached for her hand and started back up the hill, pulling her along behind him. As soon as they reached the top, he released her hand and turned to stare down the ravine at the Cobra.

"We've called a tow truck for your car, Mr. Stewart," the younger policeman said. "It should be here any time now."

"Thank you."

"After you have everything taken care of here, we'd like you to stop by the station to sign some papers," he added.

Janet hugged herself against the cold as she eavesdropped on their exchange. In the distance, she saw the promised tow truck approaching. The cast of characters expands, she thought grimly. The only one missing in their little drama was Louie. *Louie!* "Officer—" She reached out to tug on his sleeve. "If you'll take me to the corner of Market and Second Street, I think I can clear all of this up without any of us having to go to the station."

"Oh?" he replied, obviously not believing her, but listening anyway.

"That's where I was supposed to take the car after I repossessed it." She could not let go of the possibility that what had happened this evening was simply a case of mistaken identity. She had to believe that somewhere in San Francisco there was a man who fitted Eric Stewart's description who also happened to own a Shelby Cobra and was delinquent on his payments. "Louie is there right now waiting for me. I'm sure he can explain all of this."

"I thought you'd never met this Louie."

"I haven't."

"Then how will you know him?"

His condescending tone rankled and his logic hurt.

"I . . . don't know," she reluctantly admitted.

"Ms Franklin, are you aware that in the State of California, people who repossess cars must be licensed?"

The hole she was in had just grown a foot deeper. "Everyone, or just the person who owns the business?" But she already knew the answer. Casey would never have asked her to take the car if she had known a license was needed.

"*Everyone* who repossesses a car."

"I see," she said softly.

The tow truck screeched to a stop beside them, and a burly, gray-haired man leaned out the window. "Where's the car you want towed?" he asked, addressing them all.

Eric answered, a pained expression on his face. "Down there."

Janet looked at him. For an instant their eyes met. She was relieved to see the anger that had been there earlier had left the dark depths of his eyes and that he no longer looked at her as if she were an escapee from a mental hospital. "I'm sorry," she silently mouthed, not knowing what else to say to him.

Eric stared at her. Although she was as tall as the policeman beside her, with an aura that insisted she could take care of herself, she had somehow evoked a protective instinct in him.

Janet was about to reiterate her offer to pay for the damages, but before she could say anything, she was being guided to the patrol car. As they drove away, she cast one last look back. She was surprised to see Eric still standing beside the road watching her leave. Au-

tomatically her hand rose to wave goodbye. She saw
him shake his head and would have sworn there was a
hint of a smile on his lips.

The ride to the station was a lesson in humility. Separated from the front seat and her captors by heavy wire
mesh and trapped in her cubicle by doors without han-
dles, she felt as if she had already been tried, convicted
and sentenced. She looked out at the familiar surroundings they were passing, trying to concentrate on
anything and everything but her predicament and what
would happen when they reached the station. "How did
you find us so fast?" she asked. Conversation, any
conversation was better than the oppressive silence.

The older policeman, who was driving, answered
her. "Someone saw your lights when you went over the
embankment and flagged us down."

Janet plucked a piece of grass from her sweat pants.
"How long does something like this usually take?"

He eyed her in the rearview mirror. "I couldn't tell
you. We don't get many cases like this."

"Am I under arrest?"

"Not yet."

"But I will be?" Since she had been old enough to remember, the only fear she had ever acknowledged was
of the unknown. She was convinced she could handle
anything that came her way as long as she knew what
it was.

"That depends."

She could feel his impatience mounting; still she
plunged ahead. "On what?"

"On how you answer the detective's questions."

"You mean whether he believes me?"

"Precisely."

"Do you?"

"Look, lady, I don't think you really want to know how I feel about someone who does what you did to a car like that."

She leaned back against the vinyl seat cover and mentally groaned. Her future flashed before her in banner headlines—Woman's Life Ruined Doing Favor For Friend.

THE DETECTIVE assigned to question her contrasted sharply with her preconceived image of him. Not only was he meticulously groomed, but he was articulate and soft spoken as well as exceedingly polite. With swatches of gray at his temples and a sage look in his eyes, he reminded Janet of her warmhearted uncle who lived in Wisconsin and never forgot her birthday.

After introducing himself, he led her into a small conference room and offered to get her something to drink. She said a cup of coffee would be nice. When he returned with the coffee he sat down across from her at the table.

Janet wrapped her hands around the Styrofoam cup. "Detective McMillan, I have to tell you that this interview is nothing like I expected. Television has sure given you guys a bum rap."

He laughed. "We save the rooms with the straight-backed chairs and bare light bulbs for the hardened criminal types."

She gave him a hesitant smile. No matter how amicable he was, Janet couldn't forget he had the power to arrest her. "Did I hear the sergeant correctly when he said you had worked on a case similar to this one last month?" she asked, impatient to get started.

"Before I go into that, why don't you tell me what happened tonight.... Begin at the beginning."

She did, only this time, she left out none of the details, no matter how minor. Detective McMillan listened, occasionally taking notes, infrequently stopping her with a clarifying question. When she was finished, she anxiously prodded, "Well, what do you think?"

He leaned back in his chair and lightly tapped his pencil against the Formica tabletop. "I think this Louie is a very clever character."

He believed her! Janet felt as if a monstrous weight had been lifted off her shoulders.

"I've been working this detail for almost two years and thought I had reached the point where I'd seen every scam possible, but this guy has come up with a new one."

"You mean you think Louie is a thief?" Casey was going to come unglued when she found out.

"Technically, no. It looks like he protects himself by recruiting naive young women to do the actual stealing—"

How nice that he had used the word "naive" instead of "stupid," which was how she felt.

"—and then he simply steps forward to receive the stolen property."

Janet swallowed the last of her coffee. "Since you believe my story, does that mean I can go home now?"

"I'd like to run over some of the details again, if you don't mind, and then I see no reason why you couldn't go home, as long as you weren't thinking about leaving the state any time soon." There was a teasing twinkle in his eyes.

Janet went over the story twice more, gave the detective Casey's address and telephone number and finally was told she could leave. Her faith in the legal system restored, Janet bounded through the lobby of the police station on her way to find a bus to take her back to the Presidio and her car. As she stepped out onto the sidewalk, she was surprised to see Eric Stewart standing beside the curb, apparently looking for a cab. Her first thought was to go back inside the station and wait there until he was gone. Deciding that was a cowardly way to behave toward someone she had just learned had done her a monumental favor, she took in a lungful of crisp air, squared her shoulders, walked over to the curb and tapped him on the shoulder. "We seem to keep running into each other."

He stared at her for a moment before an easy, lopsided grin tugged up the corner of his mouth. "After all the years I've lived in San Francisco and *not* met you, it seems that twice in one day should be beyond the realm of probability."

"The detective told me you declined to sign a complaint."

He shrugged. "I figured your story was crazy enough to be the truth."

"I want you to know that I meant what I said about paying for your car."

Sincerity radiated from her like heat from a glowing coal. He had no doubt that she had every intention of reimbursing him, but he was just as sure she had no idea how much money was involved, "I've decided it would be easier all around if I were to turn the claim into my own insurance company, so don't worry about it."

"But how can you? Won't they. . ."

She wasn't going to make it easy for him. "Because of the kind of car it is, I have a policy that covers me for any possibility."

"Then let me at least pay the deductible."

"All right," he said, realizing that what she was really asking for was an opportunity to atone.

She waited expectantly. "Well . . . how much is it?"

"A thousand dollars."

Janet fought to hide her shock. *A thousand dollars!* Where . . . how, was she ever going to come up with that kind of money? Stalling for time to collect her wits, she shifted her weight from one foot to the other and tucked a stray strand of hair behind her ear. "I hope it will be all right if I pay you off a little at a time?"

A taxi pulled over to the curb. "As I said before, it isn't necessary that you pay me at all." He started to get into the cab. "Can I give you a lift somewhere?"

She shook her head. If taxis had been a luxury before, they were downright decadent now. "No thank you. I'll take the bus."

Eric's pragmatic side told him to cut his losses and forget he'd ever met Janet Franklin. His emotional side, which surfaced at odd moments, refused to let him drive off and abandon her alone in the middle of the night in a rundown part of town. "Get in," he said. "It's stupid for you to wait around here for a bus when I'm going right by the Presidio."

Still she hesitated. "I only have two dollars on me. . . ."

"For God's sake, will you just get in?" He was suddenly, overwhelmingly sorry he hadn't simply told her he had a fifty dollar deductible. Something told him she would pay off every cent of the thousand if it took her twenty years. And if he was certain of nothing else this evening, he was certain he did not want to be connected to Janet Franklin for twenty years, no matter how tenuous the tie.

Finally she yielded to reasoning and joined him in the cab. After traveling several blocks in silence Janet asked, "Why are you being so nice to me? I don't think I would be as nice to you if the situation were reversed."

"It probably has something to do with my genes." No one in his family had ever been able to sustain their anger longer than half an hour, no matter what the provocation.

"Your jeans?" All she needed was for him to turn out to be some kind of weirdo.

"Probably passed down from my father's side."

"Oh, you mean *genes*," she said, obviously relieved.

He eyed her. "That's what I said."

- "I thought you meant—oh, never mind."

They lapsed back into silence. This time it was Eric who broached the question. "You're in school?"

"Uh-huh." They had stopped for a red light, and Janet was staring at a young girl standing on the corner dressed in black pants and a fluorescent green shirt. Her hair was a bright orange. Since becoming friends with Earthquake, she no longer stereotyped people who had aberrant dress styles and found it fun to speculate about them.

"San Francisco State?"

"Stanford."

He was suitably impressed. Just getting into Stanford was a coup of sorts. There were hundreds of qualified applicants turned away for every one that was accepted. "Doing graduate work?"

She turned to face him, a resigned smile on her lips. She was used to people assuming she was completing her college education. "Not yet. I'm only a sophomore. I got off to a late start."

He studied her. Even without makeup and her hair pulled back into a youthful ponytail, she was obviously beyond the teen years. Her vibrantly expressive blue eyes had a knowing, mature look, which appealed to him far more than the look of an ingenue. "It must be difficult—going back to school after being away for so many years." The question was the appropriate and logical one to keep the flow of conversation going, but Eric found he was more than politely interested in her answer.

"It's not too bad now. But my freshman year was something else. I felt like I was trying to row upstream."

He chuckled in commiseration. "And scared to death to stop to rest, because you knew you'd be swept away."

"How did you know?"

"That's the way I felt my first year in law school."

"You're a *lawyer*?" There was a decided lack of enthusiasm in her voice.

Because it had happened so many times before, Eric knew what panicked thoughts were racing through her mind. She had probably already pictured herself deeply enmeshed in a lengthy lawsuit. "Corporate, not criminal."

She let out a deep sigh. "Thank—"

The taxi driver interrupted her. "What part of the Presidio?" he asked.

Janet turned her attention to the driver to give him instructions. Within minutes they were parked beside her Volkswagen. Before she stepped out of the taxi, she dug into the pocket of her sweatpants, withdrew two neatly folded dollar bills and handed them to Eric.

He looked at her outstretched hand and, sensing it was futile to resist, took the money from her.

"I'll add the rest to the thousand I owe you," she said.

"Somehow I thought you would say that." He absently wrapped the bills around his finger.

"Well . . . I'm sure you'll understand if I say it hasn't been a real pleasure meeting you." She held out her hand. A twinkle lighted her eyes.

He took her hand in his. "I understand . . . and concur."

She was out of the cab and about to close the door when she remembered she didn't know where to send the money she owed him. "Where do you live?"

"Why?" he asked suspiciously.

She laughed. "There are no hidden ulterior motives, I assure you. I just need to know where to send my payments to you."

He considered the options and settled on the San Francisco house. "One-seven-two-three Sea Cliff Avenue," he said in a rush, wishing he had told her his insurance didn't have a deductible.

"One-seven-three-two—"

"No, it's two-three." He reached for his wallet. "Never mind that address." He took out a business card and handed it to her. "You can send the money to my office. But please be sure you mark the envelope 'personal,' or the accounting department will go crazy trying to find your file."

"Right." She gave him a little salute as she backed away and reached for the door. Abruptly she stopped and bent down to peer into the cab again. "One more thing . . . I sure appreciate the way you've—"

"Don't mention it."

"Well . . . I guess I'll say good-night, then."

"Good night, Ms Franklin."

"Janet."

"Good night, Janet."

She grinned. "I'll be in touch." The door failed to close completely, so she tried again. The second time she succeeded.

The taxi driver started to pull away. "Wait a minute," Eric said. "I want to be sure she gets away all right." He watched as she dug her key out of her pocket and unlocked the car door. Even wearing no makeup, dressed in a baggy institutional-gray sweat suit and with her hair slicked straight back, she was a beautiful woman. Beautiful and incredibly gullible. He couldn't fathom how anyone could be talked into doing something so dangerously stupid.

The Volkswagen's engine coughed a puff of smoke, sputtered and popped before finally settling into its own peculiar rhythmic cadence. Eric cast one last glance in Janet's direction, then told the driver they could leave. He settled back against the seat for the drive to Sausalito, fleetingly wondering what it would have been like to have met Janet Franklin under different circumstances.

3

BY THE TIME Janet arrived home in Palo Alto, she was so tired that all she could think of was a bath and bed. Shakespeare, she decided, would have to wait until morning. Her mouth wide with a yawn, she aimed her key for the lock. The door swung open before she made contact. "Carol," she said, startled. "What are you doing up so late?"

"Are you all right?"

"As far as I know, I am." A trickle of fear dripped down Janet's spine. Normally easygoing and wise beyond her twenty-nine years, Carol Turner had faced being a widow and single parent with unfailing courage. To see her with a look of panic on her face now was unsettling.

"Then why are the police looking for you?"

She groaned. "Already?"

Carol grabbed her arm. "Would you please get in here and tell me what's going on."

"I'd really rather let it wait until tomorrow."

"Fat chance." Carol led her over to the sofa. "Now sit down and put your feet up. I'll get you a cup of coffee."

Janet knew it was useless to protest, so she settled in and reached for a throw pillow to stuff behind her head, uncovering a cache of Leggo. She smiled. Brian, Carol's four-year-old, had some strange ideas about picking up after himself. He figured as long as a toy was out of sight, it should be out of mind. Amy, the six-year-old, was the complete opposite. So much so, that Carol sometimes expressed concern over the child's almost compulsive neatness. Although only four when her father died, Amy had tried on and off since then to shoulder some of Carol's responsibilities. Wisely, Carol firmly and lovingly insisted Amy remain a little girl.

Janet leaned back against the cushion and closed her eyes. Before moving in with Carol, Janet had had little experience with children Brian and Amy's age because she was the youngest child of four. Her arrangement with Carol—twenty hours of child care a week to enable Carol to complete her master's degree, in exchange for room and board—had worked out better than either had dared to hope a year and a half ago. Instead of an employer, employee relationship, they had developed a friendship they were convinced would last them a lifetime.

Through her fog of fatigue, Janet heard Carol walk back into the room carrying a tray holding china cups that rattled against their saucers. Janet opened her eyes just wide enough to watch. Tall, blond and willowy, Carol turned heads wherever she went, but despite constant encouragement from friends, she refused to return to a social life that included dating. "You said the police called?"

"A detective McMillan."

"Did he say what he wanted?" She leaned forward to accept the cup of coffee Carol had poured for her.

"Something about not being able to reach Casey at the number you gave him. He wants you to call him."

"Tonight?"

"Only if you got here before two o'clock." She sat down opposite Janet in one of a matching set of Queen

Anne chairs and softly blew on her steaming coffee. "Now would you mind telling me what this is all about?"

Janet leaned forward and let out a sigh. Since it was already two-thirty, the call would have to wait until tomorrow. As succinctly as possible, she relayed the highlights of the evening.

Carol sat quietly through the telling, transfixed by the tale. When Janet finished, she asked, "What was he like . . . the man with the car?"

Several seconds elapsed while Janet considered the question. She summoned up a mental picture of Eric Stewart. "He's tall, has an athletic build, dark brown hair, teeth a dentist dreams about, and a funny, kind of lopsided way of walking. Probably his best feature, though, is his eyes. They're amazingly expressive. When we were down at the bottom of that ravine and he was glaring at me through the car window, all I had to do was look at his eyes, and I knew exactly what he was thinking. I have a feeling when he turns on the charm, women swoon at his feet."

"My, my . . ."

Janet looked up from the bottom of her cup to see Carol grinning at her. "What's that all about?"

"Could it be you're a little taken with this Eric guy?"

Janet's mouth flew open. "You've got to be kidding."

"All I wanted to know was how Mr. Stewart behaved after having his car stolen and wrecked, and what I got was a groupie's description of Julio Iglesias."

A wave of heat washed over Janet's cheeks. "I . . . I misunderstood you."

"Obviously." Carol began gathering their cups. "Maybe it's a good thing the deductible was so large. It will give you plenty of opportunity to see him again."

"Seeing Eric Stewart again is the *last* thing I want to do."

"Are you sure?"

"I've never been so sure of anything."

Carol gave her a sly smile. "Methinks thou dost protest too much."

Shakespeare! "Couldn't you have quoted someone else?" Janet groaned, taking the tray and heading for the kitchen.

Carol laughed. "Would you have preferred Byron?"

"I think something from Poe might be more appropriate."

Carol followed her into the kitchen. She struck a dramatic pose and lowered her voice. "Once upon a midnight dreary, while I pondered weak and weary..."

"Now that's more like it." They put away the sugar and cream and washed their cups before calling it a night. As Janet left Carol and walked down the hall to her bedroom, she thought about the mistake she had made when asked about Eric. That she had described him physically instead of detailing his actions was nothing more than the result of a simple misunderstanding. Still . . . she was bemused that she had rattled on as she had. She had meant what she had told Carol, though. In spite of his physical attributes, seeing Eric again was the last thing she wanted to do. Besides, he undoubtedly thought her a dingbat, and she had neither the time nor the inclination to try to prove him wrong.

AFTER DROPPING JANET OFF the night before, Eric had decided to stay in town rather than go home across the Bay to Sausalito. The house on Sea Cliff had been in his family for three generations. He now shared it with his grandparents, parents and sister on a cooperative basis. Rarely, however, were all of them there at the same time. Since his father's retirement, his parents had discovered the joys of traveling and were always off exploring some new country. His grandparents preferred the warmth of Palm Springs, and his sister, Susan, was a pilot for an international courier service and spent more time in the Orient than she did in the States. Eric stayed overnight at the two-story Tudor-style brick house whenever he was in the city late or had an early meeting the next day.

Though there weren't any meetings that morning, there was plenty to do. He had to make arrangements to have the Cobra towed over to Sam's Body Shop, contact his insurance agent and arrange to use the limousine service the firm kept on retainer for as long as it took to get the car fixed. He had used cabs the last time his car was in the shop, which had turned out to be one headache after another. Because he rarely remembered to check to see how much cash he was carrying, he was constantly arriving someplace and discovering he didn't have enough money to pay the fare.

As soon as the office opened, he called his secretary and had her shift his nine o'clock appointment to the afternoon. He then started working on getting the Cobra repaired. Two hours later he put in a call to Elizabeth Goodson to tell her there would be a slight change in their plans for the opera that Saturday.

Eric, Elizabeth and Walt Goodson, Elizabeth's husband, had been friends since first grade and, except for the years spent away at separate colleges, had seen each other on a regular basis since. Elizabeth worked out of her home as a free-lance interior designer. Walt managed the women's ready-to-wear department at Neiman-Marcus.

"Eric," Elizabeth exclaimed, her voice filled with sunshine. "What's up?"

"I called to see if I could get you to leave that shiftless husband of yours and run away with me to Fiji."

"Hmm . . . run away with me to Fiji. Catchy. Why don't you see if you could set it to music? Maybe we could get the maestro to include it in next year's light opera schedule."

"With you singing tenor."

"And you soprano."

"Walt could carry a sword. . . ."

She laughed. "Not around me, he couldn't. He took half his chin off again this morning while he was shaving. It's reached the point that I don't trust him around anything sharper than his finger. Lately he's been like an accident that's just waiting to happen."

Eric cleared his throat. "Speaking of accidents. . ." He proceeded to tell he about the Cobra.

"Eric, that's terrible," she commiserated. "And after you just got it out of the shop. What are you going to tell your dad?"

"If I'm lucky, he'll never find out. I figure that since he's still in Japan and doesn't know I picked the car up from the first accident, all I have to do is keep my mouth shut, and he'll think the repairs took longer than first predicted."

"Sneaky."

"What he doesn't know can't affect his blood pressure." Eric glanced at the clock on the mantel. "I'd better tell you the real reason I called before I have to hang up and get going. Since I have to use a limo these next few weeks, I thought we might as well take advantage of the service this Saturday night."

"How wonderful! You mean I finally get a chance to see how the other half lives?"

Elizabeth greeted each new experience with the enthusiasm of a child turned loose in a candy store. Eric laughed. "I won't be back from Monterey until late on Saturday, so if you don't mind, I'll have the driver go to your place first. Then you and Walt can stop by Sandra's to pick her up on your way over here."

The relationship he had with Sandra Winslow was basically one of convenience. They called on each other when an occasion required a date or, like the upcoming Saturday evening, when one of them happened to have an extra ticket.

"Walt tells me you may be losing the pleasure of Sandra's company soon."

"She has until the end of the month to make up her mind whether to accept the promotion and move to Dallas. I hate to see her go, but it's a hell of an opportunity."

"Frankly, I'd welcome her leaving."

"I thought you liked Sandra."

"Oh, I do. But I figure as long as she's around, you'll never meet anyone you might become serious about."

"Trust me on this one, Elizabeth. When the right woman comes along, nothing—not Sandra, not the entire front line of the Forty-niner football team—will stand in my way. Until then, Sandra Winslow is a perfect companion—beautiful, charming, intelligent and determined not to get involved. What more could I ask?"

"How about someone to snuggle up to on cold nights?"

It was a conversation they had had, in one form or another, a hundred times before. An incurable romantic, Elizabeth was frustrated because Eric was nearing thirty-five and still unmarried. "Trust me, Elizabeth, keeping warm on cold nights has never been a particular problem."

"I was talking about something a little more permanent."

He laughed. "I'll see you Saturday." He told her goodbye, took one last look around the room to be sure he wasn't forgetting anything, and left for the office, eager to get on with his day.

FIVE DAYS AFTER she had wrecked Eric Stewart's car, Janet was back in San Francisco, expertly maneuvering a sleek limousine through the chaotic Market Street traffic. She signaled a left turn onto Van Ness, which would take her to Lombard and then to Divisadero, where she was to pick up a client. At her request, the dispatcher at Coachman Limousine Service had given her one assignment that would last the entire evening rather than three or four by-the-hour clients. Although the tips weren't as high this way, the downtime, while she waited for her group to eat dinner or attend a show, would allow her to catch up on her homework.

Even though she hadn't had to go back to the police station that week, it had been nerve-racking waiting for a call. After learning that all Detective McMillan had wanted the night he'd called was to confirm Casey's telephone number, Janet had breathed a little easier. Now it was simply a matter of waiting for the other shoe to fall while the police and then the district attorney did his work.

As she neared Divisadero, Janet glanced at the address, which lay beside her on the seat, and calculated that the house should be up three blocks and on the right side of the street. As she made the turn, she glanced ahead to check for parking and then in her rearview mirror for patrol cars. She soon found the house, which was a light yellow California stucco and so close to its neighbors that it looked attached. It was three stories high, and the bottom level was a double garage that faced the street. With parking places as rare as the gold that had originally drawn settlers to San Francisco, a garage so large in a neighborhood such as this one could double the price of the house.

Janet pulled up to the curb, blocking two driveways and a tow-away sign. Once again, she checked for patrol cars before tucking her hair under her chauffeur's hat and heading for the front door.

A man and woman Janet guessed to be in their early thirties met her at the door. The type of pleasantries exchanged on their way back to the limousine let Janet know the evening would be a good one. She had learned she could make such judgments almost instantly from the customer's attitude toward her when she picked them up. These people saw her simply as someone doing a job, not as their servant for the evening.

After spending a few minutes showing them how to operate the television and the bar, Janet took off to pick up the next member of the party. A short time later, she was on North Point Street near Fisherman's Wharf at a high-rise apartment house that faced the Bay. As she pulled under the blue canvas portico, a uniformed doorman came over to the car. "I'm here to pick up a Ms Winslow," Janet told him.

"I'll inform her you're here."

As she waited, Janet tapped her fingers against the steering wheel, keeping time to the soft rock music on the radio. Periodically she glanced at the large glass doors, watching for a woman who was dressed as if she were going to spend an evening at the opera. When she appeared, she was wearing a shimmering silver lamé dress that clung to her perfectly proportioned body like a second skin. Janet hopped out of the car to open the door.

After greeting her two friends in the car, the woman spoke to Janet. "There will be one more stop," she said, her words spoken in a deep sultry tone, a perfect accompaniment to the dress.

"Yes, ma'am." Janet had figured as much. This was not the kind of woman who went anywhere alone. "The address?"

"One-seven-two-three Sea Cliff Avenue."

Janet silently repeated the address several times to set it in her mind. It had a strangely familiar ring. She quickly searched her memory. Between her chauffeuring job and the one at the Anything Goes Agency, she had been on assignments to every corner of the city. It didn't surprise her that an address sounded familiar, only that she couldn't remember why or when she had been there before.

Cutting across Lombard, she turned up California, puzzling over her inability to recall having been to the Sea Cliff address. As she drove the forty-odd blocks and the shops gave way to houses that became more and more expensive, Janet felt her stomach tighten and her throat go dry. With sudden clarity she remembered why the Sea Cliff address sounded so familiar. It was where Eric Stewart lived.

She felt the color drain from her face. Her heart pounded heavily in her chest. *This couldn't be happening.* She didn't believe in coincidences, so how was this incredible one possible? Out of all the limousine services in San Francisco, and out of all the drivers who worked for those limousine services, how could she be on her way to pick up the one person in the entire San Francisco peninsula whom she had hoped never to see again as long as she lived?

And then there it was—his house—sitting in the middle of the block, a short half-circle driveway leading up to the front door. Large and stately in comparison to those surrounding it, the house exuded wealth. In San Francisco, almost every piece of property held a higher premium than any building sitting on it possibly could and Eric Stewart's house was not an exception. Sea Cliff Avenue was located on the South Bay with the Pacific Ocean on its left, and the mouth of San Francisco Bay and the Golden Gate Bridge on its right. The view from the homes actually located on the cliff, as Eric's was, was so spectacular that living there would be well worth enduring the legendary fog and wind.

Janet flicked the turn signal and waited for a car to pass, grateful for the few extra seconds that it gave her to think. At least one thing was on her side: wearing a chauffeur's uniform gave her a certain amount of anonymity. She had discovered a long time ago that people who rented limousines rarely paid attention to the driver.

She had delayed as long as she could; there wasn't another car in sight. Easing the limo over the curb, she pulled into the driveway. *Oh, no,* she inwardly groaned, looking up and seeing the door open. She wasn't even going to be allowed the time it took to walk to the front door to compose herself. Frantically she checked to make sure her hair was still safely tucked under her hat. With a firm tug on the bill, she pulled the hat as far down her forehead as it would go. Despite her rush to get ready, Eric was almost to the car before she could get out to open the door for him.

"Good evening," he said politely, his voice warm and friendly.

Janet dropped her chin, trying to block his view of her face with the shiny patent leather bill on her hat. "Good evening, sir," she replied, intently staring at his shoes.

Eric hesitated. "I don't think we've met before. No, I'm sure we haven't—you're the first woman chauffeur the Coachman people have ever sent." He held out his hand. "I'm Eric Stewart."

Why couldn't he have turned out to be one of those social snobs who wouldn't dream of introducing themselves to the hired help? She put her hand in his. The contact was electric. "Ms . . . Baily, Mr. Stewart." In addition to borrowing her mother's maiden name, she dropped her voice and dredged up the memory of a southern accent she had simulated years ago in a high school play. "I hope you'll enjoy your evening. If there's anything extra I can do for you, please let me know."

"Thank you, I will." He bent over to get into the car.

In her rush to end their contact, Janet closed the door so quickly she almost caught his foot. But her relief was short lived. As soon as she returned to the driver's seat, the glass panel separating her from the passenger's compartment opened. "Since we're a little early," a now painfully familiar voice said, "we've decided to stop by

Jason's for a drink before the opera. Do you know how to get there?"

"Are you referring to the Jason's on O'Farrell?"

"That's the one."

Because he left the separating panel open, it was impossible for Janet not to eavesdrop on the back seat conversation as she drove across town. The gentle teasing and easy laughter told her that her four passengers were old and good friends. Just as she was lulled into thinking her fears about a disastrous evening were groundless, someone mentioned the Cobra.

Eric groaned. "If you don't mind, I would rather we talked about *anything* else. Between the police, the insurance agent and the repair shop, I feel like I've gone ten rounds this week."

"Well, I hope they put that stupid woman back in jail where she belongs. She's a menace." Sandra Winslow's voice was sharply disapproving.

Janet bristled. What a cretinous, unthinking thing to say. She instantly regretted every kind thought she had had about the woman in silver lamé.

"I thought I explained all that to you," Eric said.

"You did. But I fully expected that by now the police would have shot that woman's crazy story full of holes. It was hard enough to believe a detective bought her story, but when you told me you fell for it, too, I was . . . well, frankly, I was flabbergasted."

Janet glanced in the rearview mirror and saw Eric give Sandra a silencing motion. "I guess you had to be there at the time."

It was everything Janet could do to keep her mouth shut. She tried counting to ten and then to twenty. By the time she pulled up to Jason's, she was nearing two thousand.

Later, after she'd dropped Eric and his party off at the opera and had joined the other drivers and limousines that were waiting a block away, she dug her biology textbook out from under the seat and opened it to chapter seven. She was halfway through the chapter before she stopped long enough to acknowledge that she hadn't the vaguest idea what she had read. Although her gaze had swept the page, her mind had been focussed on Eric Stewart. Seeing him again had evoked a reaction wildly out of proportion to anything she would, or could, have imagined. She had thought him moderately attractive in his maroon sweat suit, but in a black tuxedo, he was nothing short of magnificent. He was one of those rare men who look completely at ease in formal clothing—someone who could dance all night and then casually discard his tie, unbutton his shirt, roll up his pant legs and stroll along a beach to watch the sunrise.

As Janet let out a wistful sigh, she caught a glimpse of herself reflected in the window and was surprised to see how vulnerable she looked. Because she was usually too tired or too busy for anything as unproductive as daydreams, it had been months since she had consciously fantasized about a man . . . any man. To have now chosen Eric Stewart as a fantasy object was a powerful indication of just how myopic she had become about work and school. What she needed was a good fixation on a movie, or rock star—someone safe—a person she couldn't possibly ever meet.

Two and a half hours later, Eric directed her to a late-night restaurant where the foursome had reservations for dinner. Two hours after that, she drove them home. First she dropped off the Goodsons, next the Silver Lamé. While Janet waited in the car, Eric escorted Sandra to her apartment. He stayed away for what turned out to be an exceedingly long fifteen minutes. As Janet watched the dashboard clock, she tried to convince herself that the minutes seemed like hours because she was tired and hungry and wanted to go home. Her impatience, she assured herself, had absolutely nothing to do with her curiosity about what method he happened to be using to say good-night.

Part of her frustration over the long wait was due to the fact that she considered herself an astute judge of character. She had decided Sandra Winslow wasn't the right woman for Eric. Sandra was a North Pole type— someone who would decorate their apartment white on white, and have one of those organized closets in which everything had its own little cubby hole and all the shoes were lined up, their toes pointing straight out like soldiers at attention. What Eric needed was someone tropical—someone colorful and casual who would balance out his own North Pole characteristics. He had had sense enough to choose friends who were that way, why not a lover? She was unconsciously and impatiently tapping her fingers against the steering wheel, chiding herself for caring how long he took to say good-night, when Eric suddenly appeared beside her.

"Don't get out," he told her, walking around to the other side of the car.

She only had a few seconds to puzzle over his actions when his intentions became clear. He was going to ride home in the front seat with her! "Mr. Stewart," she sputtered, "you can't . . . company policy doesn't allow—"

"What's this?" He held up the biology book he had found on the seat between them.

"Mr. Stewart . . . you're not supposed—" His gaze locked on her eyes, and she was transfixed, unable to break the contact.

When he spoke to her again, his voice lost all formality, becoming friendly instead, with a hint of intimacy. "I thought we decided to use first names the other night, Janet."

Her mouth dropped open. "You know? When did you . . . ?"

He reached over to tip her hat back on her head. "Almost from the beginning. Even us corporate-lawyer types are trained to be observant." He smiled. "But then your actions were a dead giveaway."

"Why didn't you say something before now?"

"Like?"

"'Good evening, Ms Franklin,' would have been good for openers."

He twisted in the seat so that he faced her. "Somehow your behavior led me to believe you preferred to remain incognito."

Needing something physical to do to help her hide her embarrassment, she started the car and pulled out into the sparse late-evening traffic. They had gone less than a block by the time a smile was tugging at her mouth. "I was afraid of what you might do if you found out I was your driver."

"I have to admit I was a little nervous the first few miles," he teased gently. "But after it became obvious you knew how to handle *this* car, I settled right down. By the way, your newly acquired accent is charming," he added, holding the book he had found on the seat up to the light to read its title. "Doing double duty tonight?"

She decided to ignore the crack about the accent. "One of the main reasons I took this job was because of the amount of free time I have to study while I wait for customers. That, and the good pay."

"You said you're a sophomore?"

"Uh-huh."

"Whatever inspired you to start school—"

"So late in life?"

"I wouldn't exactly call—" He studied her face. "What are you, about twenty-seven, twenty-eight?"

"Twenty-seven."

"Though twenty-seven isn't late, I'm willing to bet you're a little older than most sophomores at Stanford."

She had a standard flip reply to Eric's implied question, but she decided he deserved better. He seemed genuinely interested. Uncharacteristically—she rarely revealed her inner self to people she hardly knew—she told him her story.

"I fell in love when I was still young enough to believe in fairy tales and 'they lived happily ever after' endings. Robert and I were married right out of high school. The plan was that I would get a job and would work full-time while Robert went to college. We had an understanding that as soon as he finished school, I would go. Well, I worked and he went to school and everything went along according to plan. Only when he received his bachelor's degree, he decided he really couldn't get anywhere in business without a master's, which would take two more years. By this time we couldn't make it on my income alone, so Robert got a part-time job. With both of us working and Robert going to school, it finally reached the point that we only saw each other a few hours each week." She shrugged.

"Finally he got his degree, and we had some free time to spend together. It took us less than two months to discover we had nothing in common anymore. After a little soul-searching, we decided it would be best if we went our separate ways."

"So now you're putting yourself through school?" The lawyer in him recoiled. It seemed grossly unfair that she had fulfilled her part of their bargain and Robert hadn't.

Janet flashed him a knowing smile. "Robert wanted to help, but I told him I'd rather do it on my own. That way, all the strings would be broken, and we could part friends. Besides, I didn't want to be a financial drain on him if he should happen to meet someone else someday."

Eric stared at her. What she had told him seemed almost suspiciously generous. "You're a . . . remarkable person."

"No, I'm not—just practical." She smiled. "You have to remember that at the time Robert and I separated, I had no idea I would be accepted at Stanford. If I had, I might have reconsidered his offer. When we were divorced, the budget I'd figured for myself was one third what it turned out I'd need." The last thing she wanted was to sound like Pitiful Pearl. "But then it all turned out okay after all. I qualified for grants and scholarships I hadn't counted on, so with a little careful planning, I get by."

They traveled awhile in companionable silence. "What are you studying?" Eric asked, breaking the silence.

She glanced at him, trying to judge what his reaction would be to her answer. She was sure her reply wouldn't make sense to him. Few people understood her thinking. Those who came the closest said she belonged in another decade, back with the flower children of the sixties or seventies. "I'm majoring in education. I want to teach high school in a ghetto."

He took a minute to absorb the information. "Why a ghetto?"

"No speech about wasting all that money going to Stanford when I could get my teaching credentials at a State University for a tenth the cost?"

"It never occurred to me."

Trying to decide if he were putting her on, she glanced over to see if she could read his expression. It had been a long time since she had shared her dream with anyone. It was tempting. "I believe a wasted mind is a tragedy, and that education is the road out of poverty."

"I see."

She had forgotten one of the main reasons she rarely spoke about her dream. Whenever she tried to put her feelings into words, she invariably came off sounding like the Florence Nightingale of the classroom—a combination of bland and nauseatingly sweet—mayonnaise on white bread, honey on sticky buns. "I want to make a difference in children's lives." Oh great! Now she sounded as if she was on a power play! It was useless. How could she hope to make someone who lived in the rarefied world of corporate law understand about teaching in ghettos?

"What inspired you to want to teach?"

She had reached his house. She pulled into the driveway and turned off the engine before answering him. "A lot of people have asked me that." Most of them with scarcely hidden incredulity, she might have added. "I keep meaning to come up with some dynamite story, something filled with inspiration and pathos that would really impress people, but I haven't gotten around to it yet."

"I'll settle for the truth."

She shrugged. "Frustration, I guess. The welfare cycle is one of those things that everyone talks about, but no one actually does anything about—kind of like the weather."

"I think it's an admirable—"

"Oh, please, don't," she groaned. "I'm neither admirable nor remarkable, just a little crazy and a whole lot stubborn."

"How about thirsty?"

"Pardon me?"

"Would you like to come in for a drink?"

It was on the tip of her tongue to say yes, but her sensible side reigned in her enthusiasm. She already liked him too much; adding fuel to the fire would be just plain dumb. "I really shouldn't.... They're expecting me back at the shop."

"I almost forgot." Of course she wouldn't want to stay. She had put in a long day and was undoubtedly anxious to get home.

As her last official duty of the night, Janet got out of the car and went around to open Eric's door. "I hope you'll think of Coachman the next time you have need for a limousine service," she said with a formal little bow, a twinkle in her eye.

Eric reached into his pocket to get his wallet. "Damn—" he said, suddenly remembering. "I forgot to go to the bank yesterday." He gestured helplessly, acutely embarrassed. "I don't have any money...."

Janet couldn't resist. "If you're in a pinch, I could loan you a few dollars."

"No . . . that's not what I meant."

He looked so stricken she decided to let him off the hook. "If you're worried about a tip, why don't you take it off what I owe you?"

He stared at her for several seconds. "Are you sure you can't come inside?"

"I'd better not." Slowly she closed the door. Despite the damp chill of the air, she felt warm.

Eric held out his hand. "It's been fun. I'm glad we had a chance to meet under less . . . shall we say, trying, circumstances."

Her hand, given in friendship this time, fit easily and comfortably into his. "Me, too."

He walked her to the other side of the car and opened her door. "Drive carefully."

"I always do." She laughed lightly. She started the car, looked up again, smiled and waved goodbye.

Eric stepped onto the porch and returned her wave. He waited until she had reached the end of the block before he went inside. The house seemed unusually quiet and empty as he closed the door behind him. His heels tapping against the tile floor made a hollow vacant sound. Normally he was content to be alone. Tonight he wished he had company in the cavernous old house. He thought about Janet as he tossed his keys onto the hall table and went into the living room to fix himself a drink. She intrigued him. He liked tenacity in people—and gutsiness.

He wandered over to the window to watch a ship as it headed into the bay, his hand cradling a brandy snifter containing a generous splash of the golden-brown liquid. The seed of his deep-seated wanderlust, long in conflict with the practical side of his personality, had found fertile ground in the hours he had spent in front of this window as a child. The ships that entered and left the bay had seemed magically free to an eight-year-old boy confined to a house perched on the edge of a cliff. For four years, while his parents and grandparents and doctors and nurses hovered over him, their demeanors always carefully optimistic, he had lived a secret life filled with all the adventures he could imagine as he mentally sailed with the ships he watched emerge from under the Golden Gate. Someday he would fulfill the promise he had made to himself as a child. He would sail to those places of his dreams.

He raised the glass to take a sip of the now-warmed brandy. What a shock it would be for his colleagues the day he announced he was taking a hiatus from corporate law to sail around the world. "Surely not the staid, dependable, never-miss-an-appointment Eric Stewart," they would undoubtedly say. But then, their surprise would be his fault; he had given few clues of the vagabond that lurked inside the sober lawyer.

A sudden overwhelming desire to be on his boat in Sausalito struck him. The two-masted sailing vessel, still a few years shy of full restoration, was his real home. The hours he spent refinishing and restoring *The Promise* were a puzzle to his friends and family, who were unaware of his eventual plans for the ship. He preferred that they think him a little strange for wanting to live on a boat, rather than crazy, for premeditating an absence from his career. It was easier that way. Besides, how could anyone who hadn't spent all those years with his nose pressed to a window, watching ships sail away to adventure, understand what drove him to sail his own?

Tenacity—precisely what he liked in Janet Franklin. He swallowed the last of his brandy and turned away from the window. A slow smile curved his lips as he walked across the thick wool carpet to return the glass to the bar. Tenacity was definitely a plus, but Janet's long legs, blue eyes and thick black hair weren't exactly chopped liver.

IT NEVER FAILED. Every time Janet was in full makeup, her nose itched. At least twice a month, when her turn rolled around, she would spend an hour carefully applying the exaggerated smile and thick black eyebrows and then, the instant she plopped the pink wig on her head, her nose would start its thing. Being a clown was hard enough work without added irritations.

It was a glorious sunshiny Tuesday, and apart from her itchy nose and a parking ticket, the day had gone well. Since nine o'clock that morning, she had delivered twenty-eight dozen balloons to places all over the city—balloons that said everything from "get well" to "bon voyage." And the tips had been even better than normal, which meant she had enough money to make her first official payment to Eric. She had planned to mail him a check, but when her last delivery turned out to be in the heart of the financial district, she decided she might as well drop the money at his office and save the postage.

Pulling into a space reserved for deliveries, Janet took Eric's business card out of the glove compartment and stuffed it in her pocket, then hopped out of her Volkswagen and opened the trunk, where she kept all the paraphernalia connected with her job. With well-practiced motions, she fit a balloon over the end of the compressed helium tank and filled it with gas. After tying the end of the balloon in a knot, she added a string and a big red bow. Her visit to the building was going to look official.

She entered the lobby and, as usual, people turned to stare. She didn't mind. After the dozens of times she had already worn the wildly exaggerated makeup, bright pink wig and a baggy suit with big polka dots and ruffles for cuffs, she was used to being stared at. The costume instilled a peculiar kind of bravado in her. Since she was convinced her own mother wouldn't recognize her, she felt freed from her usual inhibitions. Dressed as she was, she could walk up to a grumpy-looking executive or a crying child with equal ease and would apply the same effort to making them smile. The job had given her insight into how an actor, painfully shy offstage, could work up the courage to perform in front of thousands of people.

Still, for all her boldness, she would not have come to Eric's office in costume if, on the way to the opera, she hadn't overheard him tell the Goodsons that he would be out of town this week. He already had reason enough to think she was a little strange; the last thing she needed was to give him confirmation.

As she waited for the elevator, she slipped his card out of her pocket. Eric Stewart . . . Brannigan, Andrew, Schench & Stewart . . . Attorneys at Law . . . Suite 2536 . . . The Embarcadero. Impressive. She ran her finger across the names to feel the heavy embossing. Opulence was subtly but plainly stated in the quality of the printing and paper.

When the elevator doors swung open she hesitated. Perhaps it wasn't such a good idea for her to show up in a conservative lawyer's office in a clown costume after all. She and Eric were on friendly terms now, and she might be risking bungling that friendship by chasing away his sober-minded clients. But the question of whether to enter the elevator was decided for her when she was bumped and jostled forward by those who knew where they were going and had no time for those who did not.

Watching the floor numbers flash on the indicator in front of her, she thought, *what the heck*. She'd walk into his office, hand the envelope to the receptionist and be right back out the door again before anyone had a chance to notice her.

At last the number twenty-five flashed on the tiny screen, and she stepped out into a hallway. On the wall opposite the elevator was a list of suite numbers, with arrows indicating their direction. Eric's office was to the left. Halfway down the hall, she found a set of double doors discreetly lettered with the firm's name. Unconsciously Janet patted her wig and straightened her costume before reaching for the doorknob and entering.

The office was everything she had expected it to be— all glass and brass with forest-green, knee-deep carpeting and eggshell-white sofas and chairs. The paintings on the walls were originals, and she was sure the bronzes on the tables were Bennetts. In her garish costume, she felt as out of place as a whale in Kansas.

Now that she was already inside, the only thing she could do was guts it out. Holding her chin at a jaunty angle, she squared her shoulders and waded through the ridiculously plush carpeting. "I have a delivery for Mr. Stewart," she said to the perfectly coiffed, stunningly dressed Loni Anderson look-alike sitting behind the receptionist's desk.

"Just a moment, I'll get him for you."

Janet let out an involuntary squeak of alarm; her eyes grew wide. "He's here?"

"I believe so. At least he was fifteen minutes ago."

Janet's panache deserted her. "He was supposed to be out of town this week."

The receptionist's eyes narrowed suspiciously. "You said something about a delivery?"

"Delivery? Oh . . . yes, I did, didn't I? Just a moment." In her haste to dig the envelope from her pocket, Janet dropped it on the floor. As she made a grab for it, she accidently let go of the balloon. Retrieving the envelope, she said, "Here," and handed it to the woman. Without waiting for a reply or a receipt, she headed for the door.

"Ma'am?"

Janet turned. "Yes?"

"Your balloon?"

"Oh . . ." She hurried back across the room and reached for the dangling string just as the door that led to the attorneys' offices opened and Eric stepped out. Dressed in a charcoal-gray, three-piece pin-striped suit and carrying a sleek black Porsche briefcase, he looked every inch the high-powered lawyer.

Janet mentally groaned. Of all the harebrained ideas she had ever had, coming to Eric's office dressed in bright pink and orange polka dots easily make the top ten. Her mouth went dry; she tried to swallow. She was trapped. Panicked thoughts raced through her mind. Though she was confident she could make it out the door without Eric recognizing her, she knew the minute he opened the envelope he would realize who had brought it.

Her momentary hesitation was just enough for Eric to get a good look at the features beneath the grease-paint. "Janet?"

Her heart sank to her toes. How—when no one else could have—had he recognized her? "What are you doing here?" she sighed.

"I work here."

"But you're supposed to be out of town."

"The trip was canceled." His gaze quickly swept over her, taking in everything from the big red bows on her shoes to the butterfly in her pink hair. "Now it's my turn. What are you doing here?"

"I was in the neighborhood, so I thought I would drop off a payment." She reached up to take the string, which dangled between them. "I was just on my way out, so if you'll excuse me . . ."

He reached out to take the string and, in doing so, covered her hand with his own. Glancing at the balloon, he said, "Is this for me?"

Above their heads, the bright pink balloon announced, Get Well Soon. "I wasn't aware you'd been sick, but if the sentiment applies, by all means, please take it." She was acutely conscious of the receptionist watching them and listening to their ludicrous conversation.

"Do you have time for a cup of coffee?"

"Now?" she whispered. "Dressed like this? You've got to be kidding."

"Come on." He took her hand and started back the way he had come.

"Eric . . . I can't go in there looking like this."

"Why not?" He looked genuinely puzzled.

"What will your clients think? Worse yet . . . your partners?"

"Who cares?" He gave her hand a gentle reassuring squeeze, then lead her down a long hallway, past another reception area with several women working behind desks and into his office. Propriety was the last thing on his mind. All he could think about was how good seeing her again had made him feel. He wasn't about to let her get away. "What can I get for you?" he asked, laying his briefcase on his cleared desk. "Coffee? Tea? Or would you rather have a drink?"

"Coffee would be fine."

He pressed the button on his intercom. "Would you please bring in two coffees?" While he waited, he perched on the corner of his desk and stared at her. "How have you been?"

Trying to decide whether she was in the middle of a particularly vivid dream, Janet slowly walked the length of the room, stopping beside a wall of windows that gave a panoramic view of San Francisco Bay. Eric had been a frequent, uninvited visitor to her dreams lately, so she wasn't surprised he was with her now. *That was the problem; she was absolutely sure she wasn't dreaming.* "You're not even going to ask me what I'm doing in this getup?"

"If I had to take a wild guess, I'd say you work for one of those companies that delivers balloons instead of flowers."

She gave him an exasperated look. "Doesn't anything phase you?" Suddenly, not only did her nose itch, but so did her head. She felt as if she were breaking out in hives. She hated wearing wigs. Unable to stand the torment any longer, she tried slipping a finger in under the elasticized band that held the wig to her head, but she couldn't reach the spot. Finally, in frustration, she yanked the tightly coiled polyester curls off and gave her whole head a satisfying scratch.

Eric smiled at the incongruously beautiful and whimsical picture she made. Her raven hair shone brilliantly in the late-afternoon sunlight coming through the window; her eyes sparkled through the layers of makeup, and her body moved gracefully inside the voluminous polka-dot material of her costume. "You have to realize that I was raised in San Francisco—there isn't much I haven't seen."

There was a light tapping on the door. "Come in," Eric said.

A distinguished-looking woman in her mid-fifties entered, carrying a tray with a silver coffee service. She took it over to a sideboard. "Shall I pour the coffee for you, Mr. Stewart?"

"No, thank you, Mrs. Lucas. I'll handle it."

Janet pointedly watched Eric's secretary. Not even a slightly raised eyebrow, she noted, feeling impressed by the woman's calm acceptance of the fact that a clown was in her boss's office. Janet wondered whether Eric dealt with so many eccentric clients that odd-looking people were the norm rather than the exception or if the people who worked for him were so well bred that they wouldn't dream of showing surprise at her unorthodox appearance. Either way, she would have been more comfortable with an honest look of surprise.

"Cream?" Eric asked when they were again alone.

"Black is fine." She took the fine china cup and saucer from him. As she started to take a sip, she realized what a mess her makeup would leave on the cup. "Is there somewhere I could wash this off?" She indicated her face.

Eric gave her instructions to the women's lounge. This time when she walked through the reception area, she caught one of the secretaries staring at her. So they were human, after all.

Normally she removed her makeup with cold cream. Today, she would have used a scraper to get it off. After several washes and rinses, which gave her complexion a rosy glow, she was finally satisfied. She tried finger combing her hair but decided it was a lost cause and headed back to Eric's office.

As she entered, Eric looked up from some papers he was reading. "Quite a transformation," he said, an appreciative spark lighting his eyes.

"I never should have come here dressed like this," she said, giving voice to the thought preying on her mind.

"You could have been dressed like a gorilla, and I wouldn't have minded." He had had no idea how much he'd wanted to see her again until he'd opened the door and there she was. "How have you been?" He unbuttoned his coat and leaned back in his chair.

Janet stuffed her hands in her pockets, nervously ballooning her baggy suit as she tugged on the material. "Fine...and you?" Suddenly bits and pieces of the dreams she had been having the past week came floating back into her memory. Walks on beaches... candlelight dinners... slow, clinging dances in the moonlight...lips...caresses... She felt her face crimson and quickly looked away.

"Except for a little lingering stiffness from a broken leg I had a while back, I've felt better lately than I have in a long time." Recently his days had seemed somehow brighter and filled with expectation. "How is your friend Casey? Did everything work out all right when the police got in touch with her?"

Grateful for the distraction, Janet concentrated her thoughts on her friend. She smiled at the memory. Just as she had predicted, Casey had come unglued when she'd found out she had been working for a ring of professional car thieves. "Thanks to Casey's propensity for detail, the police not only have Louie in custody, they have a complete description of every car she ever 'repossessed' for him, including the license plate numbers. The district attorney's office is delighted with her." She picked up her coffee and took a sip, grimaced and put it down again. "I waited too long, I guess."

Eric got up to pour her a fresh cup. "Do you have any plans for dinner tonight?" he asked impulsively.

Janet blinked. Had she heard him right? Was he asking her to go to dinner with him? "I . . . uh . . . I have a tuna fish sandwich down in the car."

He smiled easily. "Do you suppose I could talk you into forsaking the tuna fish and going out with me?" His heart was beating so loudly that he was surprised she didn't comment on the noise. "I assume you have other clothes with you?"

"Yes . . . I do." He couldn't have surprised her more if he'd opened the window and asked her to jump out. "But I can't have dinner with you." She looked at her watch. "I have to be to work in less than half an hour." With careful planning and quite a bit of juggling, she had arranged her class schedule this semester so that her Tuesdays and Thursdays were free. That enabled her to work her two jobs in the city back to back. It made for long days, sometimes sixteen hours or more, but it saved a lot of travel time.

Disappointment stabbed through Eric. "Tomorrow, then?"

Tomorrow she took care of Brian and Amy from three until ten o'clock. "Tomorrow's bad, too."

"Friday?"

In order to earn as much money as she could to pay Eric, she had agreed to take over one of the other drivers' late-night shifts at Coachman's this coming Friday even though she desperately needed the time for study. Quickly she went over her schedule for the upcoming week and then for the next. She gave Eric an apologetic smile. "How about a week from Friday?" she said, her flustered state making her answer sound flippant.

A week from Friday was ten days away. She obviously wasn't as anxious to see him as he was to see her. Deciding it was better to give her an opportunity to back out graciously rather than force the issue, Eric returned her smile and said, "I've never been turned down so creatively."

It was on the tip of her tongue to protest that she hadn't turned him down, when something stopped her. It was pure insanity to let anything get started between them. Eric was distracting enough in her fantasies. She hadn't the time nor energy to cope with him in reality. "Thank you for understanding." She almost choked on the words.

"Janet . . . don't kill yourself trying to pay me back. I'm in no hurry for the money."

"I know . . . I'll just feel a lot better when everything is taken care of between us." She really should leave. As it was, she would have to hit every light to be to work on time. She started toward the door. "Thanks for the coffee."

"Anytime."

She jumped when he reached behind her to open the door. If nothing else convinced her that she had made the right decision, her wildly racing heart and the ache that had just burst deep inside did the trick. The way she felt at that precise moment, she would have tossed everything else aside to spend the evening with him. It was crazy. She had to get away—and fast. Thanks again, Mr. Stewart."

" 'Mr. Stewart'?"

"Eric." She suddenly realized that he intended to walk out with her. "Please don't bother; I can find my way out."

She sounded as if she were in a panic to get away from him. What could he have done to inspire such a reaction? "All right, Janet." He leaned against the door frame and watched her as she waked down the hallway. Once, before she went through the door at the end of the hall, she looked back at him, a tentative smile on her face.

Eric returned to his office, baffled by his continuing fascination with Janet Franklin. Although he had told himself he was giving her the right of refusal, he had no intention of letting that refusal prevail. He was not through with the beautiful woman with raven hair yet. Not by a long shot.

IT WAS ONE-THIRTY that night before Janet finally pulled into the driveway at Carol's house. She should have been exhausted, but she felt wide awake and knew sleep would be a long time coming. She went into the kitchen and rummaged through the refrigerator, finally settling on a glass of milk and a small bunch of grapes. When she had finished both and had washed the glass and put it away, she headed down the hall to her bedroom. As she made her way through the dark house, she was surprised to see a light shining underneath

Carol's door. Feeling an overwhelming urge for company, she hesitated only a moment before knocking.

"Come in."

Janet opened the door and looked inside. Carol was sitting in bed with a book on her propped up knees. "Is everything okay, Carol?"

Dropping her chin, Carol peered over the top of her reading glasses. "Everything's fine. Why do you ask?"

"You're usually not up this late."

"I started a new book when I went to bed and it's so good that I can't put it down."

Janet sighed. "And I'll bet it has nothing to do with biology or physics or Shakespeare. What a luxury."

"Actually it's an old-fashioned, ten-hankie love story. I'd be happy to lend it to you when I'm through. It's wonderful."

"No, thanks. The last thing I need right now is a love story."

Carol immediately honed in on Janet's wistfulness. She patted the bed beside her. "Come sit down; we'll talk about this."

"For God's sake, don't encourage me." But she went in anyway, and sat down on the foot of the bed.

After studying Janet for several seconds, Carol took her kindergarten-made bookmark from the nightstand, placed it at her page and laid the book aside. "Don't tell me—let me guess. You've seen Eric Stewart again."

"How did you know?"

"Motherhood does wondrous things for latent intuitive skills. The only thing I'm having trouble with is whether the meeting turned out good or bad. The way you look, it could be either."

"He asked me out. . . ."

"And?"

"I told him no."

"You what?"

"Well, I didn't really say no; it just sounded like I did."

A look of understanding flashed in Carol's eyes as she leaned forward and wrapped her arms around her legs. "You put him off so far into the future that he thought you weren't interested."

"That's about the size of it."

"And now you're sorry you didn't bother to explain."

She took a minute to think about her answer. "That's my problem—I don't know whether I am or not. Under anything close to normal circumstances, I would jump at the chance to go out with someone like Eric. But the way my life is now..."

"Janet, you can't possibly be planning to hibernate the entire time it takes you to get your degree."

"Before Eric appeared in my life, I hadn't given it much thought." She kicked of her shoes and pulled her legs up. "He's the first man I've thought twice about turning down. Everyone else was easy."

"Then why did you turn him down?"

"If I have to arrange time to write my folks a letter, where am I ever going to squeeze Eric into my life?"

Carol thought for a minute. "Maybe I could rearrange my schedule so you could have a night off from the kids once in a while."

"If we did, it would just make me feel guiltier than I already do. Our agreement is woefully lopsided in my favor as it is."

"You're absolutely wrong, Janet. The complete peace of mind I have, knowing you're taking care of Brian and Amy, is worth ten times your room and board. Until you have children of your own, you'll never under-stand how invaluable you are to me."

"Still, you're gone so little as it is, I wouldn't feel right if you stayed home more."

"What about next Friday and Saturday?" Carol asked, trying another tack.

Carol's mother and father were flying in from Charleston, South Carolina, to spend a week with their grandchildren before going on to Hawaii, which meant Janet would have the weekend free. "That's fine, but what about after that?" Janet reasoned. "No matter how I juggle or rearrange or try to squeeze one more thing into my schedule, it just won't fit. The timing couldn't be worse. And unless I have some long-lost relative who has put me in his will, my life is going to be exactly the same for another two and a half years—if I'm lucky enough to graduate by then, that is."

"I don't know what to tell you, Janet. You've ob-viously spent a lot of time agonizing over this al-ready."

"I have. Now, if I could just get my heart to listen to reason, I'd be doing all right."

"This guy must really be something special."

Janet smiled. "He is—or at least he seems to be. And if he's not, I'd like a chance to find out for myself." She swung her feet back onto the floor. "Now if I could just get him to agree to wait around for a couple of years while I work on my degree . . ."

"How do you know he wouldn't?"

Janet tossed a disbelieving snort over her shoulder as she headed for the door. "Be reasonable, Carol. What man would ever agree to being put on hold for that long?"

"How do you know until you ask?"

"You've been reading too many romances. This is real life." But as Janet said good-night and closed the door, she couldn't deny the nagging wish for a different answer to her dilemma. Eric Stewart was the first man since her courting days with Robert who had made her feel as if clouds were made to walk on.

5

FRESHLY SHOWERED AND SHAVED, and dressed in faded
jeans and a yellow polo shirt, Eric poured himself a cup
of the strong aromatic Turkish coffee he brewed on
weekends and climbed out onto the deck of *The Promise*. A light breeze ruffled his damp hair as he squinted
against the brilliant morning sunlight. All around him
the gulls noisily called to one another, announcing the
new day.

Earlier that year, through time and persistence and a
touch of bribery, he had finally secured a mooring at
the end of the dock—a choice position allowing him an
unrestricted view of San Francisco, which sat across the
Bay gleaming in the morning sunlight like a multi-
faceted jewel.

It had been a hectic week mentally, and he was looking forward to the hard physical labor he had planned
for this weekend. He needed something that demanded his full attention to take his mind off the intense merger negotiations he had been working on the
past month for the firm's largest client. Tearing out,
matching and replacing several strips of damaged teak
in the forward cabin would not only provide a distraction, but when finished, it would give him a sense of
satisfaction the merger never would.

Eric cherished this time of the morning on *The
Promise* for its relative quiet and solitude. Too soon the

docks would be filled with weekend sailors readying their boats for a day on the water. Then the tourists who had come to visit the shops and restaurants of Sausalito would wander over.

Compared to the neighboring yachts, which were all valued in the million-dollar range, *The Promise* was an eyesore. Built in 1937, the ninety-two-foot-long sailing ship had gallantly, if not always steadfastly, survived a string of indifferent owners and a sinking in Puget Sound. Eric had found her through a yacht broker. When he'd flown down to Long Beach to have a look, he'd fallen in love at first sight. Seeing through the years of neglect, he had known immediately that this was the ship of his dreams—the vehicle to carry him on his journey around the world.

It had taken him several months of late nights and weekends to get the smallest cabin, the galley and one of the heads restored and fully functional before he could move in. That had been nearly five years ago. Since then he had gone through the interior completely, restoring where he could, replacing when necessary and updating the navigational guidance and communications systems with state-of-the-art equipment. The engine work he had turned over to experts; everything else he had done himself. All that remained, other than some finish work in the forward cabin, was the restoration of the deck and the installation of new sails.

Footsteps on the dock behind Eric drew his attention. He glanced up and saw Elizabeth Goodson coming toward him. He smiled in pleasure. "What have I done to deserve such a delightful surprise?" he called out to her as he moved up to the bow to meet her. Elizabeth and Walt had guessed long ago what he had in mind for *The Promise* and, after helping him restore the teak walls in the master cabin last summer, had confessed that they were seriously thinking about signing on as part of the crew the day he finally set sail.

Elizabeth made a face. "What have you done?" she repeated. "I'll tell you what you did. You taught Walt to play golf."

"Not another tournament?"

She skipped down the stairs that led to the boat level of the dock and came over to *The Promise*. "Both Saturday and Sunday this time."

Eric reached for her hand to help her on board. "Shouldn't you be in the gallery cheering him on?"

"Walt said he'd hit the ball in my direction if I dared show up today. The last time I attended one of his tournaments, I wound up in hysterics when one of the men in his foursome split his pants squatting down to line up his ball." She snorted. "Those people take themselves so seriously. They didn't see the humor at all."

"Unlike we sailor types."

She flashed him a smile. "Or we artist types."

Though Elizabeth earned her living in interior design, her first love was painting. Walt had added a small studio to the back of their house, where she would disappear for hours, lost in her quest for perfection on canvas. "You and Walt should find a mutual hobby," Eric said.

"We already have one—you."

Eric laughed. "I'm honored." He slipped his arm around her shoulders and gave her a hug. "How about some coffee?"

"Is it that Turkish stuff you make that I have to scrape out of the pot?"

"If you'd rather have tea, just say so." He led her down the steps and into the galley, where he put a pot of water on to boil and then took a mug and a tea bag from the cupboard.

"How's the merger coming?" she asked, perching on a bar stool.

"Don't ask."

"That bad, huh?"

"Worse. It looks like I'll be going to Detroit next week, after all."

"Do you want me to see if I can find someone to use your ticket?"

"Damn—I forgot all about the play." Last Christmas Elizabeth had given Walt and Eric a pair of season's tickets to an improvisational theater she had helped redesign, saying it was the only way she could assure herself companionship after both of them had flatly refused to go with her. The productions had turned out to be surprisingly good, and Elizabeth had gloried in giving both of them a resounding "I told you so."

"Is there something else besides the merger that's bothering you?" She took the cover from her tea bag and reached for the mug Eric slid across the counter.

"Why do you ask?"

"There are times lately when you only seem to be half there. And it's not like you to forget dates."

Because they had been such close friends for so many years, he knew it would be useless for him to try to deny that he had something on his mind. What he had to decide at this point was whether he wanted to talk to Elizabeth about Janet. He told himself his primary reason for hesitating was his lack of anything concrete to talk about. It sounded disproportionately monumental to say he'd finally met someone who interested him, especially when he would have to add that his feelings weren't reciprocated and that he'd received no encouragement to think they ever might be.

While he had never purposely looked for someone to love, he'd never closed the door to the possibility, either. But not once had he considered it even remotely possible that he would find the woman who piqued his interest under such bizarre circumstances. Perhaps that was why he doubted his feelings and found the warm glow and stupid grin that unfailingly accompanied thoughts of her slightly suspect.

Elizabeth leaned over the counter to poke Eric's arm. "It's also not like you to get that glassy look in your eyes and silly grin on your face and drift off into another world. Now are you going to tell me what's going on?"

"I met someone who—"

"You've met a woman?" she gasped. "Are you telling me you've finally met a woman?"

Eric tilted his cup and gazed at the dark liquid at the bottom. "My God, Elizabeth, the way you're carrying on, anyone overhearing our conversation would come away thinking I'm a little strange."

"In San Francisco, who's going to care?" She wiggled back in her stool and crossed her arms over her chest. "So tell me—who is this wondrous creature?"

"Janet Franklin." He hesitated a moment, giving Elizabeth time to make the connection.

Her mouth dropped open, and her eyes grew wide. "The woman who stole your car?" she said, her tone incredulous.

"The same."

"You mean you've been seeing her all this time, and you haven't said a word? How could you?"

"Calm down." He smiled at her indignation. "If you recall, it's only been about three weeks since the car thing. During that time I've only seen her twice."

"Well, I'll be... What a sly devil you are. Here you've been dating someone, and Walt and I never suspected a thing."

He poured himself another cup of coffee and came around the counter to join her, sitting on the other bar stool. "'Dating' isn't exactly the word I would use."

"Oh?"

"I asked her out, but she put me off."

"And you accepted that? Could this be the Eric Stewart I know and love? The man who once said 'no' wasn't an answer he recognized?"

"Oh, I haven't given up. I'm just giving her some time to realize what she's missing by not going out with me."

"Uh-huh. Let's remember who you're talking to here. So tell me about her. What does she look like? Where does she work?"

"She has shoulder-length black hair and eyes that are so blue they're almost translucent. I'd guess she's probably around five-eight or so, and I'm not sure about this, but I think she's on the thin side." He took a drink of coffee. "But then I don't know why I'm telling you all this; you've seen her yourself."

Elizabeth swung the stool around so that she faced him. "I have? When?"

"She was our limousine driver the last time we went to the opera together."

She took a moment to absorb the information. "You knew that, and you still let Sandra say the things she did?"

"At that point I was only suspicious that it was Janet. Besides, since when do I have any control over what Sandra says?"

Elizabeth thoughtfully sipped her tea. "What do you mean you *think* she's thin?"

"The three times I've seen her, she's either been in a baggy sweat suit, a chauffeur's uniform or a . . ." Eric decided he would rather not try to explain the third item of apparel. "Anyway, I haven't had the opportunity to really see how she's built."

"You didn't finish."

"What do you mean?"

"The third outfit—what was it?" She gave him a wary look.

"Oh . . . that." He raised his mug to his lips. "She was wearing a clown suit," he said with a resigned sigh.

Elizabeth leaned back in her chair. "I'm not even going to ask."

"She works for one of those outfits that delivers balloons."

"Along with her job as a chauffeur?"

"Along with carrying fifteen units at Stanford." Eric felt as if he'd just been hit over the head. Not until he had spoken it aloud had the enormity of Janet's workload really struck home. How could he have been so stupid? He reconstructed the scene in his office and could have kicked himself. A week from Friday had probably been the first free time she had. *And he had turned her down thinking she was putting him off.*

Elizabeth ran her finger around the lip of her cup. "Stanford, huh? So this woman you're interested in is a coed?"

Although she had kept her voice remarkably calm, Eric knew Elizabeth well enough to recognize when she was screaming inside. He considered letting her stew for a while but didn't have the heart. "Don't panic, Elizabeth. Janet's closer to thirty than twenty."

She cast her eyes heavenward. "Thank you, God. I'm not sure I could have kept my mouth shut if you'd sent him a teenybopper to fall in love with."

Eric reached over and playfully ruffled her hair. "Did you come over here this morning to nag or to help?"

"I can only pick one?"

HANDS ON HIPS, her chin sticking out, fury radiating from her eyes, Janet stared at Ralph Cummings, manager of the Anything Goes Agency. "You know I never do these jobs. Why on earth would you schedule me to do one tonight?"

Ralph ran his hand over his bald pate and leaned forward, stubbornly planting his elbows on his desk as he stared up at her. "Let me refresh your memory, Janet. When you called to say you would be able to work tonight, you said—and I quote—'give me whatever pays the best.' In case you've forgotten, jumping out of cakes at bachelor parties commands our highest fee."

"Isn't there *anyone* else you could get to do it?"

"Believe me, if I could, I would. All the regulars are either out on jobs or home sick. The flu that's going around is killing us." He leaned back and patted his bulging belly. "And those guys at that party sure as hell ain't gonna put up with someone like me coming out of that cake."

Despite herself she smiled. She liked Ralph Cummings. He was a perfect boss, always willing to work around her schedule and arrange an extra job for her whenever she had a little free time. "I've never done anything like this before." She considered the whole idea demeaning. "I don't know the routine."

"What's to know? You wait for the cue, jump up and look sexy."

"Ugh!"

"Oh . . . there's also a little poem you're supposed to say, but it's not very long. You don't even have to memorize it, you can read it if you want to."

"*Wonderful*. Is this poetry something the agency provides, or does it come from the client?"

Ralph avoided her gaze by looking down at his desk. He cleared his throat. "This one comes from the client."

Janet's eyes narrowed. "I absolutely refuse to read anything that's obscene."

"It's not obscene—just slightly blue."

"You'll pardon me if I don't take your word on this. May I please see this poem?"

Ralph reached inside his desk, brought out a plain white envelope and handed it to her. "I've read worse," he said, a cajoling tone to his voice.

Janet took the neatly folded paper out of the envelope and began to read. As her gaze swept the page her eyes grew wide and her face turned a bright pink. When she had finished, she tossed the paper on the desk. "What does this guy do for a living—produce porno flicks?"

"All right, you don't have to read his poem. You can read the one we normally use at these things. If he complains, tell him his was lost somewhere." He got up and came around the desk. "You know I wouldn't ask you to do this if it weren't important, Janet. These people have been clients for a long time, and I would hate to lose their business."

Every ounce of her common sense told her not to take the job. "Are you *sure* there's no one else available?"

"If there were, do you think I would be down on my knees to you?"

Janet felt herself weakening. Though the agency contracted to do some crazy things, they were always in good taste. Even the men and women hired as strippers to go to offices and homes for birthday parties wound up wearing what were rather modest swimsuits once their strips were complete. Janet had already seen the outfit she would have to wear for the cake routine. Basically it was an old-fashioned black corset trimmed in red lace. She'd also be wearing black fishnet stockings and a red garter belt. But it wasn't the clothes she objected to. She had been wearing less that fateful day she'd caught pneumonia trying to pass out hors d'oeuvres to yacht customers. What she had trouble with was the idea. "How much do I get paid?" she said with a resigned sigh.

"A hundred plus tip."

"And you're sure they know we have a hands off policy at the agency?"

"It's in the agreement they signed. Plus I personally reminded them."

Janet chewed on her lower lip while she thought it over. She knew several of the women at the agency who usually took these kinds of jobs, and they had told her that though once in a while they ran into jerks who would try something, for the most part, the "honorees" were gracious and friendly. "How long do I have to stay?"

"Half hour, tops."

"Okay, Ralph, I'll do it this time—but don't you dare ever schedule me for something like this again. If you do, you'll lose the best clown you ever had." The instant the words were out of her mouth, she knew she was making a mistake.

Ralph gave her a bone-crushing hug. "Thanks, Janet. I won't forget this."

"Something tells me I won't, either."

TWO HOURS LATER, wearing a fleece-lined trench coat over her skimpy costume, Janet was wandering around the service entrance of the Beachwood Hotel, impatiently waiting for her cake to arrive. She stopped, stood as straight as possible and sucked in her breath, trying to relieve the pain in her chest caused by a plastic stay that had worked loose from the corset. When at last the delivery van pulled around the corner, she let out a sigh of relief. As soon as the men pulled up to the curb, she gave them hurried instructions on where to put the cake and excused herself to find someplace private where she could fix the stay.

The repair work turned out to be more complicated than she had anticipated, and when she returned, she discovered the delivery men were already gone. *Oh, great!* She had hoped to get them to stick around long enough to roll the cake into the banquet room—a minor detail she had neglected to work out with Ralph Cummings. She reached into her pocket to get the name of the man who had arranged the evening, then motioned for a bellboy. When he came over, she gave him the name and asked him to go into the banquet room and page him. Several minutes later a tuxedo-clad, middle-aged, balding man—his tie askew, his face flushed from alcohol—came up to her.

"What can I do for you, little lady?"

His breath and the strange way he leaned forward when he talked to her told Janet the party had been going on for quite some time already. "I'm Janet Franklin from the Anything Goes Agency." She stuck out her hand.

"Glad to meet you, Janet. I'm Bill Evans." He chortled. "But I guess you already knew that, didn't you, honey?" He took her hand and brought it to his lips to press a loud, moist kiss on the back. "The pleasure is all mine, I assure you."

Janet felt a familiar stab of certainty. "Mr. Evans, I'm going to need some help with the cake." Perhaps if she remained scrupulously professional he would respond in kind. "The men I had hoped to get to handle it have disappeared. Now if you could get a couple of your friends—preferably sober ones—out here, I can explain what I need done, and we can get on with the surprise."

"How about a little preview first?" He tried to wink but blinked instead.

"I beg your pardon."

"You know—how about letting me see what you're wearing under that coat of yours? Wouldn't want old Rick to be disappointed with the merchandise we ordered for him."

Ralph Cummings, you're a dead man, Janet vowed. She gave Bill her best withering stare. "Since 'old Rick' isn't getting any merchandise, there's not much chance he'll be disappointed, is there? Now I would suggest you get those men out here before I change my mind about doing this and go home."

He responded to her anger by giggling. "I can get you the men, but I can't get them sober," he said in a singsong voice.

Janet thought a moment. While the cake wasn't fragile, if improperly handled, it could easily be damaged. It would be very expensive to replace. "Never mind. I'll find someone myself. You go back to the party." She would just have to commandeer someone who worked for the hotel.

"Splendid idea. Why don't you walk back with me while you tell me your plans?" He started to reach out to put his arm around her, but Janet easily sidestepped him.

"All we need to do is coordinate our times for the entrance, and then you can walk back by yourself." They settled on fifteen minutes from then. She considered telling him he wouldn't be hearing his poem but doubted that, at the stage he was at, he would even notice it was missing. After he'd gone, Janet closed her eyes and tried to come up with five good excuses why she shouldn't simply walk out the front door and forget all about the party, the cake and her job.

Reason won out. It was only a half hour; she would never have to do it again; the pay was good; and though she loathed, abominated and despised the whole idea, it wasn't life threatening, illegal or immoral. Realizing it was possible for her to stand in the middle of the lobby arguing with herself all night, she cleared her mind of everything but getting the job done and headed over to the desk.

The bell captain begrudgingly loaned her two of his people after she promised the job wouldn't take more than ten minutes. She gave the two young men their instructions, took off her coat and gingerly climbed into the cake, pulling the lid down on top of her. The cavity where she waited had been built for someone considerably smaller. The fishnet stockings dug into her knees and toes, and the corset fit so tightly that she found it almost impossible to breathe. Resorting to her usual method for passing time when it seemed to go on forever, she counted the seconds, figuring that by the time she reached three hundred she should feel the cake begin to move.

ERIC STOOD at the back of the banquet room, nursing a drink and trying to look as if he were a legitimate part of the crowd. Crashing the party had been ridiculously easy. By the time he had arrived an hour before, there were few people in the hall who were sober enough to recognize their own mothers, let alone someone who didn't belong at the party.

Coming here had been a dumb idea; but after a week in Detroit, where he had spent more time thinking about Janet than about the merger he'd gone there to work on, his need to see her again had superseded common sense.

Because he'd arrived in San Francisco so late, he had called the Coachman Limousine Service from the airport instead of waiting until he got home to find out if Janet was working that night. When they told him she wasn't due to come to work again until Tuesday, he had tried to get them to give him her home telephone number, but they had adamantly refused.

Not ready to give up so easily, he then called the Anything Goes Agency. By taking a different approach and turning on his most persuasive charm, he managed to convince the receptionist that, though naturally she couldn't give out any information about where Janet lived, she would not be releasing confidential information by giving him the address where Janet would be working that night. In the flush of success, he had forgotten to ask precisely what job Janet was doing. Consequently, he had been wandering around the room, watching grown men make fools of themselves and trying to figure out what Janet could possibly be doing at a party like this one.

The groom, who appeared to be somewhere between forty and fifty and certainly old enough to know better, was slowly turning green around the gills as friend after friend proposed toasts in his honor. As the evening progressed, the jokes became more ribald and, what had at first been snickers, soon turned into roaring laughter. It was not a party that could be enjoyed by anyone remotely sober. He leaned against the wall and thoughtfully rubbed his chin. What in the hell was Janet doing with a bunch like this?

Someone at the head table took off his shoe and banged it on the table. Instead of producing the desired silence, fifty other men removed their shoes and banged them on their tables. In response, the first man crawled up on the table and stood there waving his arms. By promising a spectacular surprise if they quieted down, the rotund organizer, his shoe still clenched in his hand, managed to dull the noise. He handed his shoe to the man next to him and motioned for a drum roll, then swung his arm in a grand gesture toward the entrance.

The big double doors swung open, and a giant cake was wheeled in. A wild cheer quickly followed by a host of catcalls, each more crude than the last, greeted the cake's entrance. Eric cringed. The mystery had been solved.

ABSOLUTELY CONVINCED that she had made a mistake in ever agreeing to take the job in the first place, Janet desperately fought to capture the feeling of anonymity she had when she wore her clown costume. If she could just get through this night, she would know she could face anything. Abruptly the forward motion stopped. She tried to listen for the cue—"and now let's cut the cake"—but all she could hear were shouts, whistles and what sounded like stomping feet.

The ear-shattering noise outside, and the painfully cramped quarters inside, combined to make her feel as if the world were closing in on her. A trickle of perspiration slithered down her spine; she tried to catch her breath. Dull panic hung over her like an ominous black cloud, and "claustrophobia" became more than a word she had always had trouble spelling. *She had to get out of there.*

Through the noise, she heard a rapping on the plywood side of the cake. Convinced it had to be a signal for her to make her appearance, she reached up to throw the lid back. She forced herself to smile as she stood up, her arms thrown wide. She was almost to a full standing position before she realized there was something terribly wrong with her legs. They were like twin towers of gelatin. The time she had waited in the cake with her legs awkwardly cramped under her had put them to sleep. She made the connection too late. When she tried to sit down, she lost her balance and went tumbling over the side.

With amazing reflexes, considering his level of intoxication, the party's honoree made a grab for Janet as she fell. She landed half in, half out, of his arms. Obviously thinking it was all part of the act, he held on tight, pulling her close and nuzzling her neck.

"Put me down," Janet hissed.

He ignored her, his kisses wandering lower as he headed for the creamy mounds of flesh above the red lace trim.

"Either put me down or I'm going to—"

He cut her off with a resounding kiss on the mouth. The party goers cheered, which just egged him on.

Janet felt him begin to wobble. She tried to wriggle free. Suddenly his sloppy kisses were the least of her worries. If he didn't release her, they were both going to topple over and crash into something. Too late. They fell backward, hitting a wall that had been covered by a red velveteen drapery, then slid to the floor. For an instant they both just sat there in shock. Then the world went black as the rod was pulled from its mooring and the curtain fell, completely covering them.

Dust filled her nose and her mouth, making her cough and sneeze as she tried to untangle herself. Hands reached for her—none being any too careful what they grabbed. Unbridled laughter filled the air as if those around her had been told the world's funniest joke. Obviously they were under the impression this was all part of the act. Janet tried to stand, but her legs still wouldn't function. She looked up into a sea of grinning faces.

She was struggling to get up when confident hands touched her from behind, taking hold of her arms and raising her. When she caught her heel in the curtain and lurched sideways, she was quickly turned, lifted up and thrown over someone's shoulder. The impact jammed the corset stays into her ribs and knocked the breath out of her. She was too stunned to resist and didn't have the air to protest when she felt herself being carried out of the room. A chorus of howls, objecting to her departure, only made her rescuer move faster. Soon they were out into the fresh air of the lobby, and then, the still fresher air outside the building.

By the time they were at the end of the block, Janet had started to catch her breath and knew by the lessening of the tingling in her legs that she would be able to stand. "You can put me down now," she said, placing her hands in the small of his back and pushing, still not completely sure whether she had been rescued or kidnapped.

"Are you sure you're sober enough to stand up on your own?"

That voice! *Oh, my, God.* It couldn't be. "Put me down," she demanded indignantly. Eric bent over to drop her feet to the pavement, reached up and grabbed hold of her arms to steady her. She yanked herself free from his grasp and glared at him. "How dare you accuse me of being drunk?" she shouted, hiding her embarrassment with righteous indignation. "I'll have you know I haven't had anything to drink since last Christmas, when some idiot spiked the eggnog at a preschool party I attended." She turned and started to walk back toward the hotel. Thinking of something else she wanted to say, she whipped back around. When she saw a tolerant smile on his face, her anger multiplied. Prepared to take on the world, she stomped back to stand toe to toe with him, poking her index finger into his chest to emphasize her words. "You try jumping out of a cake with both of your legs asleep, and we'll just see—"

Eric calmly took off his jacket and started to put it around her shoulders.

"Just what do you think you're doing?" She jerked away from him.

"Stand still and let me put this on you. When you calm down a little, you'll realize it's freezing out here."

"I have a coat . . . I don't need yours."

"That's okay by me. Where is it?"

She looked past him at the hotel. "In there."

"I don't suggest we try to retrieve it right now. That bunch in there wasn't too crazy about losing you the first time. I'm not sure I could get you out again."

As if subconsciously verifying his statement about the cold, Janet abruptly started to shiver. "I suppose you're right," she reluctantly admitted. This time when Eric put his coat around her, she didn't resist. "Now what do we do?" she said, snaking her arms into the sleeves.

"Well...we could find a coffee shop somewhere and wait around until we thought it was safe enough to come back here for your things."

"There aren't many coffee shops that are going to let me in dressed like this."

"Or we could wait it out at my place." Her momentary hesitation was all the encouragement he needed. He motioned to a passing cab. "I make better coffee than you'll find in any restaurant, anyway."

After they were inside the cab and Eric had given the driver his address, a thought occurred to Janet. "How did you happen to be at that guy's party?"

"It's a long story."

"I have lots of time."

Eric stared at her. Although, as he had so recently learned by hefting her over his shoulder, she was not a small woman, she was dwarfed by his jacket. The sleeves covered all but the tips of her fingers; the length reached her knees. "I wasn't a guest. I called the Anything Goes Agency to find out where you were working tonight."

She frowned, puzzled. "Why did you do that?"

"I wanted to see you."

"And so you crashed the party?" She looked down at her lap. The whole miserable evening flashed before her in living color. She was mortified that he had seen her involved in yet another fiasco. "You certainly could have picked a better time to look me up."

"Actually, I thought my timing was pretty good. A man doesn't get many chances to come to the rescue of a lady in distress these days." He reached over and touched her chin, raising it until she was looking at him. "How'd I do?"

She met his gaze. "Not too bad—except for the sober crack." At least he had the courtesy to look chagrined.

"Please accept my most humble apologies."

A grin tugged at her mouth. "It seems to me you jumped to some pretty fast conclusions. Just because I fell out of a plywood cake into some strange man's arms and wound up on the floor covered with a moldy curtain is certainly no reason to think I was anything less than sober."

"I agree—my conclusions were inexcusable."

Janet shivered. In an impulsive gesture that surprised them both, she moved across the seat and snuggled into Eric's side, seeking his warmth. She was dumbfounded by her actions, but once she found herself there, she didn't know how to gracefully move back again, so she stayed.

Eric held his breath, afraid to touch her, afraid to move even enough to make their contact more comfortable for fear he would scare her away. That was the last thing he wanted to do. "Cold?"

"Freezing."

His hesitancy to touch her disappeared. He put his arm around her and gently brought her close. Faint lingering traces of her perfume drifted up to him. It was a fragrance he had never smelled before...floral, but not sweet. "I like your perfume," he said.

She brought her legs up to tuck them under her. "Thanks, I like it, too. A wonderful old lady made it for me last year when I delivered eighty-five balloons her grandchildren had ordered for her birthday. There were too many of them to take into her tiny shop, so we stood outside and had a wonderful time giving them away to the neighborhood children. She said it was the best birthday she'd ever had. Afterward, she took me inside her shop and made this delightful perfume blend for me. I still go by her place and have lunch with her whenever I happen to be in the neighborhood."

"It sounds like you enjoy your job."

"Most of the time I do. I like meeting and talking to people. I'm lucky, though. I almost always see them on happy occasions, so that makes them happy to see me." She stopped, trying to hold her head stiffly and not let it rest against his shoulder. "As you have probably figured out by now, jumping out of cakes isn't my forte. I make a much better clown." She had forgotten how special it could feel to have someone's arms around her. The dreams that had haunted her since meeting Eric hadn't come close to relaying how warm, how extraordinarily comforting, it would be to actually be in his arms.

"Still cold?"

"I'm better."

Eric put his other arm around her so that he was holding her as intimately as he would a lover. In response she cuddled closer still. Inside of him, Eric's emotions were having a Fourth of July celebration. Fireworks were going off in every direction without rhyme, but certainly not without reason. He still didn't understand what it was that Janet did to him. He only knew how good it made him feel to be around her. "How's school?"

"We're in the lull before midterms—that gray time when you tell yourself that if you don't know the answers by now, then cramming at the last minute won't help, but you go ahead and cram anyway."

"I remember. You try to convince yourself sleep is more important, but you stay up all night studying— just in case."

"Tell me something about you. What's it like to be a corporate lawyer?"

Eric gently rested his chin on the top of her head. "If you like maneuvering behind the scenes of large corporations, it's scintillating. Otherwise—we're the types who've been known to put people to sleep at dinner parties."

"My brother's like that."

"Boring?"

She playfully poked him in the ribs. "He'd much rather be the power behind the throne than sit there himself. In high school he always chose to be the stage director, never the star of the production, even though he was very good at that sort of thing."

"What does he do now?"

"He works for the CIA."

Eric laughed. "Somehow that doesn't surprise me."

"I'm kidding. Actually he's a hospital administrator in Bismark, North Dakota."

"Is that where you're from?"

"Uh-uh. I was born and raised in Portland, Oregon. I didn't move to California until after Robert and I were married." As naturally as if they had held each other this way a hundred times before, her arm went across his waist when she shifted in the seat to try to get more comfortable. "Sad, huh? Here I am, twenty-seven years old, and I've never traveled farther than up and down the west coast. Too bad they don't make tramp steamers anymore. I'd sign up in a flash."

A private smile tugged at Eric's mouth. "Oh, but they do," he said softly. "As a matter of fact, I happen to know of one that's going to set sail in a couple of years."

Janet tilted her head back to look up at Eric, but was prevented from questioning him further because the taxi pulled up in front of his house. They sat there entwined even after the taxi had stopped, each reluctant to be the first to break contact. Finally the moment grew awkward, and Eric was forced to let go of Janet in order to reach into his back pocket to get his wallet.

"Damn," he softly swore as he counted out the bills.

"A little short of cash?" Janet struggled to keep from smiling.

He looked at her. "Before I left Detroit I made sure I had enough money to get home from the airport...."

She reached into the top of her corset, where she had tucked her money earlier. She handed the driver a twenty-dollar bill. When he gave her the change, she handed it to Eric.

"I don't need this," he said, trying to return the money to her as they got out of the cab.

"How are you going to go someplace tomorrow to cash a check if you can't pay a cab to get you there?" she answered logically. "Besides, I feel particularly responsible for putting you into your predicament. If you had your own car, you wouldn't be taking taxis."

He grinned at her. "I like your reasoning." His arm slipped easily around her shoulders as he walked with her up to the front door. He not only liked her reasoning, he liked the way she felt beside him and the way she smelled, the way she looked—there were a lot of things he liked about Janet Franklin.

6

ERIC UNLOCKED the front door and stepped aside for Janet to enter. A soft light illuminated the entry hall. To her left was a small table, and above it an original oil painting she recognized from the art appreciation class she had taken last semester. She waited for Eric before venturing any farther. He came up behind her.

"Let's see if we can find you something to wear before I make you some of my world-famous coffee." He took her hand and led her toward the stairs at the end of the hall.

Janet had to remind herself not to gawk as they made their way up the stairs and passed yet more paintings she recognized. She had never been too good at judging such things, but she was relatively sure the art work she had already seen easily totaled more than a million dollars. The thought left her a little breathless.

Eric opened the first door on the left and motioned for Janet to enter. Decorated in mauve and burgundy, with touches of blue and white, it was a decidedly feminine room and far too elegant to belong to anyone but a grown woman. Janet mentally recoiled. Not once had it occurred to her that Eric might be married. Of course it hadn't—if he was married, why Miss Silver Lamé?

The personal touches on the dresser and the book on the nightstand left no doubt that the room was currently being used, which eliminated it as a guest room.

As she stood in the middle of the room and looked around, an avalanche of emotions swept her along on a wild ride. Disappointment, anger, disillusionment, embarrassment—each tugged her in its own direction. She didn't bother taking any time to understand her disproportionate reactions or to try to hide them. "Whose room is this?" she demanded.

Eric stuck his head out of the walk-in closet with a pair of slacks in one hand, a folded sweater in the other and a puzzled look on his face. "It belongs to Susan." When she didn't respond, he added, "My sister."

"Your sister? You live here with your sister?"

"Only sometimes. Actually, I can't remember the last time we were both here at the same time." He walked over to her. "Here, try these on. You look like you're about the same size as Susan. . . ." He gave her a teasing smile. "And she would never object to lending her wardrobe for such a good cause."

Automatically Janet reached for the clothes. Although her own basically functional and inexpensive wardrobe had been purchased at a dozen factory outlets in the San Francisco area, the two years she had spent working in an exclusive woman's apparel shop had taught her to recognize quality and had given her the ability to judge price. The sweater Eric had handed her was cashmere, and the slacks were raw silk. Together she was sure they represented close to a month's salary for her. Eric's sister would have to be an exceptional woman not to mind someone else wearing these clothes. "I'd be a lot more comfortable in jeans and a sweatshirt—if Susan has anything like that."

Eric laughed. "She does, but they're her staples. She never leaves them here when she's flying."

"Your sister's a stewardess?"

"It's a good thing she isn't here to hear you say that—it so happens she's a pilot."

Janet groaned. "I *hate* people who stereotype."

He headed for the door. "That's all right. Your secret's safe with me."

Now that comfort was only moments away, Janet was anxious to get out of the too-small corset and fishnet stockings. "Eric...thank you. For everything." She was rewarded with another smile.

"My pleasure. Now hurry up and get dressed. I'll be waiting for you in the living room."

As soon as he closed the door, she dropped the sweater and pants on the bed, slipped out of Eric's jacket and began untying the laces on her corset. Once free of the garment, she took several deep satisfying breaths and scratched her ribs where the stays had left red marks. She reached for the sweater. Holding the beautiful lavender garment in front of her, she felt her heart sink to her toes. How could someone as big as Eric have a midget for a sister? The sweater was a good two sizes too small for her. She reached for the pants and held them up to her waist. They were stylishly short, hitting her at midcalf. The only problem was that they had been cut to be shoe length.

She was confident that if she struggled and forsook breathing and never sat down, she could squeeze into the sweater and pants. But they would be ruined after she was through with them. Eric must never have really looked at her to think she would be able to wear his sister's clothes. Begrudgingly she put the corset back on and went downstairs. She met Eric coming out of the kitchen.

"What's wrong?" he said. "Why haven't you changed?"

She grabbed his hand and led him into the living room where he had turned on the lights. At first she just stood there, her hands on her hips, at a loss for words. Finally her emotions found voice. "Would you please look at me?"

"What?"

"I want you to take a good look at me and tell me what you see."

She was so agitated that he decided not to question her further. He backed up and complied with her request. Slowly his gaze traveled her body, taking in everything from the way her breasts mounded softly above the red lace on the corset to the narrowness of her waist to the graceful length of her shapely legs, which were accentuated both by the heels she wore and the almost hip-high cut of the corset. The expression on his face reflected his thoughts as they changed from curiosity at her strange request to open admiration of her statuesque build.

The natural progression of his thoughts created a stirring inside him that nearly took his breath away. His eyes met Janet's, and he knew she had witnessed the transformation. It was as if they had suddenly been stripped of all ability to camouflage their true emotions and were laid bare to each other's eyes. Under the trappings of civilization and social mores, the ancient, basic drive that had perpetuated mankind since the beginning of time still smoldered in them. When fanned to flame, its power was staggering.

Janet swallowed. Her heart beat heavily in her chest. She struggled to breathe. What passed between them seemed imbued with a power of its own—to control and possibly to destroy the fragile relationship they had established. It was too soon for these feelings to surface so blatantly. Their defensive shields gone, they were far too vulnerable.

Eric struggled for a semblance of normalcy, feeling he was in the middle of a battle to preserve the budding friendship they had managed to establish. He forced himself to stop looking at her, dropping his gaze to the floor and reaching up to rub the back of his neck. Nothing like this had ever happened to him before. Never had he felt a desire for a woman that precluded every rational thought. Its effect left him shaken. "I . . . made us some coffee," he said, fighting to reestablish some kind of stability between them.

Janet hugged herself. "I . . . uh, thank you. Would . . . uh, would it be all right if I used your phone?"

Eric looked up, staring into her eyes, trying to read them. Was she seeking a way to get away from him? "Of course—it's in the study." He pointed to an open door at the end of the hallway. When she moved to step around him, he reached out to take her arm. "Why did you ask me to do that—to look at you?"

Unable to meet his gaze any longer, Janet stared at the front of his shirt, inconsequentially noting a thread working its way loose from a buttonhole. "I couldn't believe you had ever really looked at me before."

Oh, the answer he could have given her. Not only had he looked at her, but her image had become his constant companion when they were apart. Her presence in his thoughts was radically disproportionate to the time they had spent together and the relationship they had established. "I don't understand."

"Your sister must be half my size." Now she did look at him. She wanted to see his reaction. "How could you possibly think we could wear the same clothing?" Only then did she realize the intensity of her feelings stemmed from her keen disappointment. Subconsciously she must have hoped that he had woven her into the fiber of his days as completely as she had him.

"Since it's certainly not you—it must have been my sister I've never really looked at all these years," he said softly, understanding at last.

Slowly, as radiantly as a flower opening to the warmth of a morning sun, Janet smiled. "I'd better call Ralph Cummings and tell him what happened at the party before someone else gets to him first."

He moved aside to let her pass. "As soon as you're through I'll let you try on something of my mother's— she's a lot closer to your size—and I promise you, I have looked at her often enough to know."

"Your mother? She lives here, too?"

"Along with my father . . . and occasionally, my grandparents."

Eric had never moved away from home? She thought a second. "I don't think I know—"

"About any grown man who still lives with his parents?" There was a teasing look in his eyes. "That was what you were about to say, wasn't it?"

"Uh . . . that's not precisely what I was going to say." It was close enough.

Eric slipped his arm around her shoulders and walked with her to the study, purposely striving to recapture the easy familiarity they'd had before they had been thrown for such an unanticipated loop. On the way he explained the function the San Francisco house served for his family. "So you see, it's not quite as bad as it first sounded."

"You didn't have to explain."

"I figured it was best to get everything out in the open just in case you wound up having to try on my grand-mother's clothes if my mother's didn't fit."

She leaned lightly into his shoulder. "So where do you really live?"

"First make your phone call, then we'll talk when you get through." Eric closed the door behind him when he left.

Janet walked across the room to the massive oak desk that sat in the corner facing the window. She perched on the edge of the desk, reached for the phone and dialed. "Ralph—this is Janet."

"I already know what you're going to say."

She crossed her legs and leaned her elbows on her knees. "Who told you?"

"The guy who originally hired us. He called to con-gratulate the agency for coming up with such a clever comic routine—said it was a lot more fun than any he's ever seen. I'm not completely convinced he's still going to feel the same way in the morning. But tonight he's well pleased with what he got for his money."

"I can't believe he's not mad." Janet was flabber-gasted. In her wildest imaginings she couldn't have come up with this scenario.

"Believe it—he's just concerned about getting your tip to you." Ralph chuckled. "He did mention that we might want to consider changing the routine a little and have you come back for a final bow. I told him we'd take it under consideration."

"And how do you feel about all this?"

"Before *I* tell you that—*you* tell me how the cake looks."

"I don't know. I didn't get much of a chance to see it on my way out, and then I didn't go back inside to check on it for fear I'd never be able to escape again. But since I have to go back to the hotel to get my things later, I'll be able to check it out and give you a call."

"Was it really as bad as it sounded?"

The highlights of the evening flashed in front of her eyes like an old-time movie—full of stops and starts and jerky action. Now that it was over, she was able to laugh at the memory. "I think it was probably worse than you heard, Ralph. The groom and I were rolling around on the floor with this great big curtain wrapped around us. I was sneezing and he was choking. Everyone else was laughing. . . ."

"Are you all right now?"

"I'm fine."

"Listen, don't worry about the cake, I'll send someone over for it later. If it's damaged, it's damaged. There's nothing we can do about it anyway. Go home and get some sleep, and I'll see you tomorrow."

She almost groaned aloud. "I thought I had tomorrow off."

"Just a minute, let me check here. You're right, you do have the day off. I guess I won't see you until Tuesday. Well, enjoy your weekend."

"Thanks Ralph, you too." She said goodbye, replaced the receiver and had started to leave when the phone rang. Without thinking, she picked it up.

"Is Eric Stewart there?"

"Just a second, I'll get him for you." She went to the door to call Eric. He came into the study to take the call, and she started to leave, but he stopped her by taking her hand.

"This is Eric Stewart," he said. When he recognized the caller, his shoulders slumped in weariness. "Howard, do you have any idea what time it is? I realize that, but just because it's two hours earlier out here doesn't mean it's not late. Besides, it's Friday night. I told you I would call you first thing Monday morning, just as soon as I had time to research those items we discussed."

Janet was beginning to get cold again. She gently tugged her hand free, pointed to the other room and then to herself and mimed drinking a cup of coffee.

"Hold on a minute, Howard." He put his hand over the mouthpiece. "I'm sorry, Janet, I'll get rid of him as quickly as I can."

"Don't worry about it . . . I'll get myself some coffee and wait for you in the living room."

"Thanks."

She smiled and gave him a thumbs-up signal as she left. Before getting her coffee, she made a detour upstairs to retrieve Eric's coat. Despite being inside, she was still cold. On the way into the kitchen, she caught a reflection of herself in the plate-glass windows of the living room. The French twist she had used to put her hair up earlier had started to come apart, releasing one long strand of hair that bobbed when she moved her head. As she reached up to tuck it back in place, she was struck by the cumulative image of the woman staring back at her. She closed her eyes and let out a soft groan. She looked like a hooker. And a cheap one to boot!

What if Eric's sister happened to choose tonight to return to San Francisco? Or his parents? Or, God forbid, his grandparents? Resolutely she turned away and headed for the kitchen. Since there was nothing she could do about the way she looked, the next best thing was to ignore it.

After rummaging through three cupboards, she found a cup and went over to the counter to pour herself some coffee. With the evening winding down, fatigue had begun to settle over her like a giant invisible shawl, first on her shoulders, then gently covering the rest of her. She had been up since four o'clock that morning and had gone to bed at one-thirty the night before. She leaned back against the door frame and spent a second inhaling the fragrant steam from the coffee before taking a sip. She made a face when the bitter black liquid hit her tongue.

Eric's "world-famous coffee" was unequivocally the worst thing she had ever tasted. Not even her mother, who was known to occasionally forget to rinse the soap out of the electric percolator before brewing another pot, had ever made coffee that tasted this bad. Janet shuddered and walked over to the sink and poured the foul liquid down the drain, checking to see if it was going to foam back up when it hit the trap. She vowed she would have to be near death in the middle of a blizzard, with Eric's coffee the only source of heat, before she would ever subject herself to it again.

She wandered back into the living room and looked around. In here the colors were primarily blue and white, with highly polished cherrywood used for the end tables and accent pieces. Built-in lighted bookshelves held several pieces of Chinese porcelain—all in distinctive blue and white. The room avoided a museum look, though, through the eclectic assortment of books haphazardly placed on the shelves and, what was obviously someone's favorite resting place, an old, nearly worn-out high-back wing chair with matching ottoman.

Since all the lights were on in the room, and the fog had rolled in earlier, she knew she wouldn't be able to see the view from the window without pressing her nose against the glass and cupping her hands around her eyes. Since that would leave telltale fingerprints all over the glass, she didn't bother trying. Besides, she really didn't have to actually look outside to know precisely what the view was like—breathtaking. This was one of the wealthy areas of San Francisco and the view the location afforded was the chief consideration in the value of the house.

Still cold despite Eric's coat and, without anything to keep her busy, becoming increasingly more aware of her fatigue, she kicked off her shoes and curled up on the corner of the couch. The house was quiet except for a softly ticking clock on the bookshelf and the traces of Eric's conversation that occasionally drifted in her direction. As she sat there waiting for him to return, her eyelids slipped farther and farther down her eyes. Whenever they closed completely, she blinked them open—which worked for a while. The first time she forgot to blink, they stayed closed....

Eric had finally reached the conclusion that there wasn't any way he could allay Howard's fears about the upcoming merger short of flying back to Detroit and holding his hand. "Howard, this is simply going to have to wait until Monday. Why don't you take the weekend off—go skiing or something. You're going to drive yourself crazy if you don't give this thing a rest for a few days."

"I couldn't relax if I did go away."

"It's not going to do you any good to stay around there stewing about this thing, because if you come up with any new questions, you're not going to be able to get in touch with me again even if you wanted to. I'm leaving tonight and will be out of town the entire weekend." It was a lie, but it was the only thing he could think of to get Howard to take a few days off and relax. He was turning into a nervous wreck, and Eric had begun to worry about his physical state.

There was a slight pause. "Are you leaving because of me?"

Eric laughed. "To be honest, the thought did cross my mind."

"I'm sorry about this, Eric. I know I'm being a pain in the—"

"Howard, I'm going to hang up on you now and check to see whether my company has decided I'm never coming back and has left to go home."

"By any chance are you talking about the woman who answered the phone?"

"Uh-huh." There were times when Eric regretted having a client who also happened to be a friend.

"You should have said something sooner. I just assumed it was Susan."

"Well, I'm saying something now—right along with goodbye."

After he had finally got rid of Howard, Eric sat at the desk a while longer, trying to compose an effective apology for leaving Janet alone for so long. While he had been growing up in this house, proper social behavior had been as integral a part of his life as the smell of salt water and the call of sea gulls. He decided to wing it, hoping she was as understanding as she seemed.

When he found her curled up on the end of the couch, sound asleep, he felt twice as guilty for spending so much time trying to pacify Howard. He knelt close to her and reached out to touch her arm.

Before his hand made contact, she let out a moan. A shiver raced down his spine. The sound she had made was the most erotic he had ever heard. He spent a moment watching her, unwilling to wake her. As he waited, he was inevitably, inexorably caught up in his own imaginings. In the guise of a shadowy, illusive figure, Janet had wandered in and out of his mind the past three weeks, both when he was sleeping and when he was awake. Though his imagining had rarely followed scripts, the emotions were always the same—powerful, demanding, enticing. And always he was left with a hunger more acute than the time before, forcing him to acknowledge that what he felt for Janet was becoming the focal point of his days and nights.

Suddenly her breath came in quick sighs, and she touched her lips with her tongue. She turned in his direction, and his coat separated. She need only move a little farther, and her breasts would be free of the gently confining lace. With unsteady hands he covered her again.

He smiled as he looked at her. She was amazing. Even in her tawdry costume, an air of elegance shone through. Somehow she managed to be impish and coolly regal at the same time. And she was beautiful in a way he seldom noticed in the women he came into contact with on a daily basis. Her clear skin, strong bone structure and the thick dark eyebrows that accentuated her incredible blue eyes made makeup superfluous. Imagining her on *The Promise* with the wind in her hair, the sun at her back and a smile meant only for him took his breath away.

His gaze dropped to her legs and he noted the way they were drawn up close to her body for warmth. She had precisely the kind of long, lean build that appealed to him—the build of someone who moved and walked with such grace that people stopped to stare...of someone born to move easily about the deck of a ship.

He was sorely tempted to get a blanket and have her spend the night where she was, but he was afraid someone might be waiting for her. Gently he touched her shoulder.

His touch seemed like a caress to Janet, and still sleeping she moved toward him, snuggling against him. He let out a sigh, and her eyes fluttered open. What happened next happened so naturally that Eric became a participant without conscious thought. All he knew was that he was suddenly holding Janet in his arms and kissing her, and that this was everything he had imagined it would be. Instantly he was thrown into a world so finely focused that everything else disappeared. The house could have been burning down around them, and he would have been oblivious. In his mind, a symphony celebrated this special moment of their coming together for the first time. *You were right*, a voice echoed in his mind. All those times he had told his family and Elizabeth and Walt that there was a special woman meant only for him, and that he would find her someday—he had been right. She felt so good—he felt so good holding her—that he never wanted to let her go.

Janet felt Eric's initial restraint disappear when she opened her mouth and encouraged the deepening of their kiss. Somewhere in her subconscious the voice of sanity called out to her, demanding she recognize precisely what she was doing. But she ignored the summons, allowing the warm swell of pleasure that filled her world with fireworks and rose petals to take precedence. It had been such a long time since she had felt a man's arms around her...so long since she had known such intense desire, and she was caught unawares by its force. Like a tree toppled into a storm-swollen river, she was swept along in the current without control, leaving reason, a shadowy figure, on the shore.

She pulled her hands from beneath the pillow and wrapped her arms around Eric's neck, effectively destroying the last of his reserve. He moved to lie beside her on the wide sofa, holding her next to him, keenly feeling the pressure of her thighs as he did so, catching his breath as her hips cradled against his own. He inhaled the scent of her, letting it fill his lungs and imprint itself forever on his mind. Touching his lips to her face, to her throat, to the gentle swell of her breasts above the straining lace, he learned and memorized the texture and feel of her skin, making it a part of himself.

Janet's hand boldly traveled from his waist to his thigh, and he mentally stepped aside as he waited to see where she would touch him next. Suddenly he understood what had just happened between them and knew he could let it go no further. Her extreme fatigue and the feelings that were growing between them had left her vulnerable and receptive. He caught her hand and brought it to his lips, already regretting what he was about to do. "I think we should stop and think about this before we go any further, don't you?"

The groan Janet let out this time had nothing to do with passion. She struggled to sit up, pressing herself deeply into the corner of the couch. "Eric . . . I'm so sorry." Wishing she could simply disappear, she covered her face with her hands. "God, I'm so embarrassed."

He reached for her hands and pulled them away. "Janet, look at me." The smile he gave her was more a wonderfully delighted lopsided grin than the reassuring one he had intended. "Do I look like I'm complaining?"

Although he was trying to make things easier for her, she saw something in his eyes that told her he knew all of her secrets as surely as if he'd been able to step into her mind. And then, as she looked at him, something else happened that totally changed things between them once more. If she had broken their eye contact a moment sooner, she would have missed the passage into his soul. As plainly as if he had spoken the words aloud, she saw the reason he so clearly understood her. He lived with the same deep need to be held and touched and loved, and he held it as tightly in check as she did.

They sat there, staring at each other, terrified by what had just occurred and yet ecstatic because of its implied promise. Eric took her hand. "I've been looking for you for a long time," he said simply. "I can't tell you what it means to me that I've finally found you." With infinite tenderness, he leaned forward and kissed her. This time their kiss was one of budding friendship. "Although what I would really like to have you do is stay," he said softly, "I think you'd better go."

She would have stayed if he had asked, but her heart swelled with gratitude that he hadn't. What was happening between them needed nurturing time to fulfill its promise. Tonight they were both shell-shocked after their explosive lovemaking. It would take a while before they would be able to deal with their feelings. "Thank you, Eric."

"I'll call us a cab."

"You don't have to go with me."

"But I want to."

She touched the side of his face and smiled. "Every week for almost two years I have wandered all over this city at all times of the day and night all by myself—and nothing has ever happened to me. Trust me—I'll be all right."

"I'd still feel better—"

"Eric—that twenty dollars I used for the first cab fare was all I had, and I only have enough gas in my car to get me back to Palo Alto. Now if you come with me, how are we going to get you back home again?"

Begrudgingly he said he saw her reasoning and agreed to let her go alone. "When do you get off work tomorrow?"

Her eyes lighted with pleasure. "It so happens, I have tomorrow off."

"Then spend it with me."

She shouldn't. She had homework she had postponed doing all week because she knew she would have Saturday free. In spite of a powerful twinge of guilt, she nodded.

"What would you like to do?"

"Surprise me."

He smiled. "It's a deal. Can you pick me up, or should I rent a car?"

"Do you think you can fit those long legs of yours into a Volkswagen bug?"

"I did all through college."

"Then we'll take my car. Where are we going?" She grinned. "Should I bring lots of money?"

He clutched his chest as if mortally wounded. When he'd recovered, he winked teasingly. "As I recall, my bug got pretty good gas mileage, so twenty dollars should do it."

Reluctantly Eric left her and phoned for a cab. While they waited he rummaged through his mother's closet until he came up with a coat that fitted her. Janet had been afraid he would come out with a full-length fur that she would be paranoid about wearing. She was delighted when he handed her a beautifully cut wool coat.

"Except for the down jackets she takes skiing, it looks like this is about the warmest thing my mother owns."

"She doesn't wear furs?" Janet asked, surprised. She tried on the coat. It fitted perfectly.

"My mother would go naked before she would wear a fur coat. She has trouble with her conscience whenever she wears leather or eats a hamburger."

Janet looked up at him. "I think I just might like your mother."

"I know she's going to like you. Now why don't I get you a cup of coffee while we wait? That way the inside of you will be warm, too."

He'd taken her by surprise, and she was stuck for an answer. "Oh . . . I already had a cup . . . when you were on the telephone. It was . . . it was really different. How in the world do you—"

"I knew you'd like it. I grind the beans myself, and I've only been able to find one shop in town where I can get them in quantity. I buy them by the case and freeze them." Before he could add anything more, a horn sounded outside. He returned Janet's money before walking with her to the door. "Tomorrow—ten o'clock?"

"I'll be here." She lingered a moment, unsure whether to kiss him goodbye. Eric took the decision out of her hands when he caught her to him in an eloquent embrace, giving her a lingering kiss that told her how reluctantly he was letting her go.

All the way to the hotel and then to Palo Alto, she had a silly grin on her face. As she let herself into the house, she decided that sometime next week she was going to have to call Casey and thank her for getting involved with a ring of car thieves. The thought made her laugh. She could just imagine Casey's reaction to a phone call like that.

7

THE NEXT DAY Janet arrived at Eric's house fifteen minutes early and knew a moment of keen disappointment when she discovered he wasn't home. She was on her way back to her car when a cab pulled up in the driveway and Eric got out, carrying two large sacks of groceries.

He gave her a wonderful smile of welcome as he strode across the lawn. Dressed in jeans and a tweed jacket, he looked younger and more carefree than Janet had seen him before. "Have you been waiting long?"

"I just got here."

"Reach into my front pocket, would you? The key for the door is in there."

Janet felt a blush warm her cheeks. "How about if I take the bags instead? Then you can get the keys yourself." She shifted his mother's coat from her arm to her shoulder and prepared to take the groceries.

He chuckled as he handed her the bags, adding shyness to the list of things he was learning about her.

"Good grief," she said, staggering under the weight. "What do you have in here?"

"Supplies for our picnic."

"And who are the other ten people we're inviting to join us?"

"Think I got a little carried away?"

"Only if we're planning to stay less than a week."

Eric opened the door and reached for the bags. "I believe in being prepared."

"You and the Boy Scouts."

"Come into the kitchen. I have a real treat in store for you."

Janet closed the door and followed him. When they neared the living room, however, she veered off in that direction, drawn to the window and the breathtaking sight of the Golden Gate Bridge spanning the mouth of San Francisco Bay. She had never seen this side of the bridge before. She stood there, mesmerized by the raw beauty of the gently rolling hills of grassland on the opposite shore and the breathtaking effect of the morning sun as it reflected off the water like millions of beckoning diamonds. Today was one of those special early winter days in San Francisco when there wasn't a trace of the area's famous fog to hamper the view. The air was so clear that it seemed feasible she could see forever.

Eric came up to stand beside her. "No wonder you never left home," she said. "If I had grown up in a house with this kind of view, I don't think I would have left, either."

"The four years I sat in front of this window when I was a kid gave me a love of the sea that has never left."

"Why only four years? If I were you I would have had my nose pressed against the glass all the time." She glanced up at him.

"I had a problem with my heart, and there were delays in arranging the necessary surgery to repair it," he stated simply, relaying none of the trauma or desperation that had controlled his family's existence back then.

"And now?" she asked softly, almost afraid to trust her voice.

He drew her to him and held her, deeply touched by the loving concern he saw in her eyes. "I'm fine." He pressed his lips against her fragrant hair in a fleeting kiss. "I even jog—remember?"

Reassured, Janet put her arms around his waist and held him tightly. "Something tells me I will never be allowed to forget that auspicious evening."

Eric chuckled. "Stand back and let me look at you," he commanded, changing the subject.

Janet readily complied, shrugging out of her coat, delighted he had thought to call attention to how carefully she had dressed that morning. She was wearing the brown light wool slacks Carol had given her last year for Christmas and the tan sweater she had found at Loehmann's to go with them. It was the best casual outfit she owned, and she willingly turned for his inspection.

"You look fantastic."

She gave a little bow. "Thank you, sir. I'm glad you approve."

"Do you realize this is the first time I've seen you dressed in what could be considered normal clothes?"

"I can't say the thought didn't occur to me once or twice this morning." Not only had it occurred to her, it had been her constant companion as she tried on every halfway suitable thing in her closet. She took his arm. "What's this surprise you have for me in the kitchen?"

"Can't you smell it?"

Instantly Janet grew wary. What she had thought she smelled when they first came in was a lingering charcoal odor—as in burned food. "I . . . I'm not very good at guessing games."

"I got up early this morning and baked chocolate chip cookies for our picnic. It's been years since I had any, and I thought maybe it might have been a while for you, too. I had to wake up my neighbor to get most of the ingredients—everything but the flour and salt to be precise." He chuckled. "It's a good thing she likes me."

He looked so pleased with himself that she didn't have the heart to tell him she had made a double batch of chocolate chip cookies for Brian and Amy just the week before. "You didn't tell me you were a man of so many talents."

He guided her into the kitchen. "Before I moved onto *The Promise*, I'd never boiled water. I've come a long way in the past few years." He guided her into the kitchen.

"Before you promised yourself what?" she repeated, losing part of his sentence in the sound of the closing door.

Eric's answer died on his lips when he looked at the table and saw that one of the bags had fallen over, spilling its contents all over the floor. "Dammit," he mumbled, angry with himself for not taking the time to be sure the bag was balanced. He bent to pick up the jars, checking them for cracks before putting them back on the table.

Janet went after a can of stuffed olives that had rolled over to the refrigerator. She took it to the counter where she discovered Eric's cookies piled high on a plate. She surreptitiously studied them. The cookies were only slightly less dark than their chocolate chips.

Eric caught her staring. "They're a little overdone, but they taste great." He took one from the plate and offered it to her.

There were too many butterflies doing their thing in her stomach to find any room for one of his cookies. "I'd better not," she said, pressing her hand to her midsection. "I had a big breakfast."

He took a bite and happily crunched away as he went back to gathering things for their picnic.

Janet fleetingly wondered if anyone had ever told him chocolate chip cookies weren't supposed to sound like toasted almonds when chewed. "Where are we going?"

"Sonoma—ever been there?"

"I don't know if I have or not. Where is it?"

He frowned, taken aback that anyone who lived in California was unaware of Sonoma. "You know . . . the place where those pushy settlers told the Spanish they were declaring California a state." When that failed to elicit a response, he tried again. "Wine country?" he prodded.

That did it. She gave him a big smile, delighted with his choice. "Fantastic. I've always wanted to go up there."

"I can't believe you've lived in California all this time and you've never been to the wine country. I thought you said you'd done the West Coast."

"I have—Portland and San Francisco."

"That's it?"

"Pretty much, except for a few miles into Washington. My folks had a cabin near Mount Saint Helens, where we went weekends and vacations."

"Did they lose the cabin in the explosion?"

"No, they were far enough away to miss the major force of the blast. They did get a ton of ash they had to clean up, though."

Excitement shot through Eric. He caught her by the waist and pulled her into his arms. "If you'll let me, I'll show you the world."

She laughed. His enthusiasm almost made her believe him. "If we don't get started, we'll never see Sonoma." It felt so good to be in his arms, she wasn't sure she really cared whether they ever left or not.

Eric stared at her; an ache filled his chest. She was so beautiful. How he wanted her... and how he would scare the hell out of her if he didn't stop his thoughts right there. "You're right," he reluctantly agreed. He lightly touched her lips with his own. It was a mistake. Instead of the simple, friendly gesture he had intended, he found himself in a desperate mental battle to keep from kissing her again. The last thing he wanted to do was let her go, but he did. He was playing for higher stakes and wasn't about to screw things up between them on their first real date by coming on like a randy teenager. "Why don't you get the basket out of the pantry, and I'll finish unpacking," he said, amazed at how calm he sounded.

Dazed by the powerful feelings Eric's simple kiss had aroused, Janet went to the other side of the kitchen and opened the pantry door. She turned on the light and stepped inside, stopping to catch her breath and calm her racing heart before reaching for the large wicker basket sitting on the top shelf.

Trying to understand and to put into perspective the impact Eric was having on her, she took a minute to think about the days when she and Robert had first dated. Had there been a time when she had felt about him the way she now felt about Eric? Had there been a point in their relationship when she'd thought the ground had been removed from beneath her or that the

entire world had gone from gray to Technicolor? Either
her memory had grown dim, or nothing like this had
ever happened to her before.

Robert had been her first real boyfriend, and she had
been painfully naive and had not understood her slow
awakening of sexual urges. She had been curious, yet
frightened by them. She was no longer naive. The stir-
rings and the longings she felt were readily identifia-
ble, though lately, not very common. Still, she was a
little frightened—not by the hunger Eric had awakened, but by its intensity. Up until last night, that hunger had only afflicted her when she was asleep and
dreaming of him. How was she ever going to cope with
something that was this consuming when she was wide
awake?

She reached up to get the basket. All Eric had done
was give her one brief kiss, and she had nearly at-
tacked him. Though she had come to think of herself
as a thoroughly modern woman, she had never tried the
role of aggressor in a relationship—both because it had
seemed unappealing and because, until she had met
Eric, there had been no one she cared that much about.
If she were to walk back into the kitchen and see the
same look in Eric's eyes, she wasn't sure what she would
do.

Grasping the basket handle, she resolutely headed
back into the kitchen. Eric was at the sink measuring
water into a glass coffeepot. He looked up when she
came over to stand beside him. "I thought I'd make us
some coffee for the thermos."

Remembering the coffee he had made the night before, she gulped. Disposing of the evidence to save his
feelings would prove far more difficult when they were
constantly together. She had been dumb to let him

think she liked the stuff in the first place. Now what was she going to do? "Coffee? In wine country?" she gasped. "Surely there must be some law against it."

He grinned. "There probably would be if the growers thought they could get away with it."

She took the pot from him and poured the water down the drain. "Let's not take a chance on upsetting the locals." To distract him, she shoved the basket in his hands. "The sooner we get going, the sooner we get there."

When she offered to help with the packing, Eric sent her back into the pantry to find a checkered tablecloth and napkins. By the time she located both, he was finished with the food and ready to go.

Two hours later they were looking for a parking place in Sonoma. As one of the oldest cities in California, the community drew visitors even in the off-season. After two more hours, in which Janet played tourist and Eric her guide, they were dodging raindrops as they ran across Sonoma Plaza on their way back to their car. Breathless and laughing, they scrambled inside, collapsing against the seats. "What incredible weather," Janet said, wiping rain from her face with the back of her hand. "I would have sworn the sun was still shining when we went into the mission."

Eric reached over to daub a raindrop from the end of her nose with the tip of his finger. "As far as I'm concerned," he said, a warm smile in his eyes, "the sun never stopped shining."

"Aw . . . what a nice thing to say."

He loved the way she looked—her cheeks flushed from the dash for the car, her eyes dancing with excitement, her mouth slightly open in innocent invitation. His thoughts strayed to the wondrous way those lips had felt when they'd been pressed against his own last night and earlier that day. He reached over to take her hand in his. "Are you hungry yet?"

"Starved."

He thought a moment. "Since it looks like we'll be having our picnic indoors, the least I can do is provide a pleasant view." He touched his lips to the back of her hand before starting the car.

From anyone else, Janet would have thought a kiss on the hand corny. From Eric it seemed natural and un-affected. "Where are we going?"

"Buena Vista Winery, where a Hungarian count by the name of Haraszthy planted California's first vine-yard. There's a pretty little creek that runs along the side of the winery, and the eucalyptus trees that grow there are some of the biggest in the state."

"How do you know so much about this area?" Eric had displayed a native's knowledge of the region and of the historical buildings they had gone through.

"Your family's not the only one that had a cabin where they went for weekends and holidays. Ours is about ten miles from here, up in the Napa Valley hills." He chuckled. "The facts and figures I have used to daz-zle you with today, however, are due to my grand-mother's persevering nature. Whenever we all happened to be at the cabin at the same time, she would insist Susan and I tramp around the countryside with her. She had decided we should have an appreciation of our heritage whether we wanted it or not."

Janet felt a twinge of envy. Her grandparents lived on the East Coast, and she had rarely seen them as a child. "Would she quiz you later?"

"She didn't have to. Susan and I were like sponges." Eric smiled at the memory. "You'd have to meet the grande dame to understand how she managed to pull it off. Grandma didn't just do show and tell, she made us touch and absorb and insisted we try to imagine ourselves as the original occupants."

"She sounds like an incredible lady."

He grinned. "Grandpa sure thought so . . . still does, as a matter of fact."

They turned onto Old Winery Road, a narrow twisting country lane with farm houses and trees along either side. By the time they had traveled two miles to the end of the road, they were at the winery. The cellars were housed in a large stone building, and picnic tables were scattered around the grounds. Eric stopped the car beside the creek. Because they were the only visitors, they had wonderful privacy as they looked around the rustic setting.

"Did you arrange for us to be here alone?" Janet asked in a joking voice, but believing it was entirely possible.

"I'd like to take the credit, but I think it was probably a combination of the season and the weather." He twisted sideways in the seat so that he could reach in the back to open the basket.

Listening to the soft sounds of rain and the ticking of the engine as it cooled, Janet felt cozy and content. It had been such a long time since she'd taken a day off to do anything as carefree and spontaneous that she had almost forgotten how good it felt. She leaned forward to stare out the window, trying to see the top of the tree in front of them.

"Huge, isn't it?" Eric handed her a napkin.

"You were right. I've never seen eucalyptus trees as big as these before." She opened the napkin and spread it across her lap, her hunger increasing in direct proportion to the nearness of the food. "By the way, I

HIT
THE JACKPOT
WITH HARLEQUIN

Scratch off the 3 windows to see if you've
HIT THE JACKPOT

If 3 hearts appear—you get an exciting
Mystery Gift in addition to our fabulous
introductory offer of

4 Free Books Plus an
Exquisite Pen & Watch Set

THE JACKPOT

Peel up Sticker
and
MAIL TODAY

IT'S A JACKPOT OF A GREAT OFFER!

- 4 exciting Harlequin novels—Free!
- an LCD digital quartz watch with leather strap—Free!
- a stylish ballpoint pen—Free!
- a surprise mystery bonus that will delight you

But wait...there's even more!

Special Extras—Free!

You'll also get our monthly newsletter, packed with news on your favorite writers, upcoming books, and more. Four times a year, you'll receive our members' magazine, *Romance Digest.* Best of all, you'll receive periodically our special-edition *Harlequin Bestsellers* to preview for ten days without charge.

Money-saving home delivery!

Join Harlequin Reader Service and enjoy the convenience of previewing new, hot-off-the-press books every month, delivered right to your home. Each book is yours for only $1.99—26¢ less per book than what you pay in stores! Great Savings plus total convenience add up to a winning combination for you!

YOUR NO-RISK GUARANTEE

- There's no obligation to buy—and the free books and gifts are yours to keep forever.
- You pay the lowest price possible and receive books before they are to appear in stores.
- You may end your subscription anytime—just write and let us know.

TAKE A CHANCE ON ROMANCE—THEN COMPLETE AND MAIL YOUR SCORECARD TO CLAIM YOUR 7 HEARTWARMING GIFTS.

PLAYER'S SCORECARD
MAIL TODAY
FREE BOOKS
Free Pen & Watch Set

Did you win a mystery gift?

PLACE STICKER HERE

☐ YES! I hit the jackpot. I have affixed my 3 hearts. Please send me my 4 Harlequin Temptation novels free, plus my free watch, free pen and free mystery gift. Then send me four books every month as they come off the press, and bill me at just $1.99 per book (26¢ less than retail), with no extra charges for shipping and handling. If I am not completely satisfied, I may return a shipment and cancel at any time. The 7 gifts remain mine to keep.

NAME

ADDRESS   APT.

CITY

PROV./STATE   POSTAL CODE/ZIP

Stylish LCD quartz watch– just one of your 7 gifts!

You'll love the appearance and accuracy of your new LCD quartz digital watch. Genuine leather strap. Replaceable battery. Perfect for day-time...elegant enough for evening. Best of all, it's just one of 7 wonderful prizes you can win— FREE! See inside for exciting details.

meant to ask you how you managed to get to the store this morning without cab fare."

Frustrated by the cramped quarters and his repeated failures to keep the can opener attached to the can, he momentarily bypassed her question. "Are you any good with can openers?"

"A whiz."

He handed her the can and the opener. "I talked the driver into taking me to the delicatessen and waiting outside while I cashed a check."

Janet licked a trickle of sauce that had spilled on her finger when she accidently tipped the can. She made a face. "What is this?" she asked suspiciously, trying to recognize familiar words on a label written in French.

"Escargot," he said, obviously surprised that she didn't recognize the taste. "The shells are back here. I even brought a fondue pot and sterno to cook them with."

Janet fought to keep from gagging. "Snails?" she choked. "We're having *snails* for lunch?"

"Not only snails," he said proudly, too occupied with the basket to notice her reaction. "I brought caviar and lox and bagels and cream cheese—"

"And potato salad and hard boiled eggs?" she added hopefully.

"No . . ." he said, looking up in time to see the panic on her face, "but there's crackers and liver pâté." He suddenly realized his selection of food had been a horrible mistake. He had thought to make the picnic wildly elegant and nonsensically fun and had even put a couple of candles and a pair of silver candlesticks in the basket. He hadn't once considered the possibility that his choice of food might be alien to her. Unwilling to let his mistake put a damper on their day, he took the partially opened can from her, wrapped a piece of plastic around it and tossed it back in the basket. "This stuff doesn't look nearly as appetizing to me now as it did when I was in the store. What say we go someplace and get ourselves a couple of nice juicy hamburgers?"

She looked down at her lap. "Oh, Eric, I feel like a—"

He caught her chin in his hand. "Stop right there," he demanded, his heart going out to her. He felt like kicking himself for creating a situation that had caused her embarrassment. He ran his thumb along the line of her jaw, his gaze caressing her. He could pretend no longer. "I absolutely refuse to let *anyone* say anything bad about the woman I think I'm falling in love with."

Janet's heart skipped a beat; she struggled to catch her breath. She couldn't believe she had heard him correctly. Unable to look at him or to let him see the flush of pleasure that had stripped away all her pretenses, she glanced out the side window while she fought to regain her composure. Finally she turned back to look at him. "Think?" she asked softly.

A slow, glorious smile lighted his eyes. He leaned forward and tenderly kissed her. "Damn near positive," he whispered against her mouth.

"Me, too," she murmured. What was she saying? This couldn't be happening; the timing was all wrong. Where, how, was she ever going to be able to fit Eric into her life? While her mind shouted denial, her arms came up from her sides and wrapped around his neck. The reality of him holding her was far superior to her dreams. The solid feel of him, the way the musky smell of his cologne filled her senses, the way his lips melded against her own in a silent message filled with longing—all were more intense, more poignant than she had been capable of imagining. She felt as if she had been calmly floating along a quiet stream before she had met him. In coming to know him, she had been pulled into rushing water, and then, with his touch, she had been tossed into a cascading rapids, from which there was no escape. "Eric..." She put her forehead against his shoulder and tried to catch her breath. "What are we doing?"

His hand trembled when he reached up to smooth her hair. He looked at the foggy windows and smiled. The image he had of himself as a fairly sophisticated man had just been shattered. The windows and the gear shift poking him in the leg were perfect representations of the way he felt—like a randy teenager at a drive-in movie. "When I thought about what we should do together today, I tried to create a situation where it would be impossible for this to happen—never once did I consider how impossible the situation would become if it did."

"Now what do we do?" she sighed.

He grasped her shoulders and gently pushed her away, then caught her chin with his hand so that she would have to look at him. He wanted to be able to judge her reaction to what he was about to say. "The cabin I told you about earlier is only about twenty minutes away from here." What they would do at the cabin was understood. It seemed forever before she answered.

A battle raged inside Janet. Her body ached for the release he offered; her mind cried out a warning that it was only a temporary solution. The frustration that would haunt them later would be a hundred times as sharp as the pleasure they would know now. But even as she was forming the words to tell him no, she said, "Yes."

Eric drew her to him. Her mouth parted in welcome, in invitation. A deep moan sounded in his throat. His lips caressed her, coming to know the feel of her eyes, her nose, her chin. She tilted her head to the side, and he traced a line down her neck. He pressed a kiss to the hollow behind her ear, inhaling the smell of her hair, tasting the sweetness of her skin, taking heady pleasure in the demanding beat of her pulse.

The way he felt, the ten miles to the cabin might as well have been a hundred. He tried to pull himself away to get started, giving her what was to be one last kiss. But it quickly turned into another and then another, with each becoming deeper, more demanding as they teetered on the brink of losing control.

Finally, with a supreme effort, he released her. He took a minute to regain a semblance of composure before he reached for the napkin on her lap and wiped the fog from the windows. When he finished, he started the car and pulled back onto Old Winery Road. "Talk to me, Janet. Say something that will make the miles go faster."

She tucked her trembling hands under her legs and gave him a lopsided grin. "We could always sing ninety-nine bottles of beer on the wall."

"Tell me a joke instead. A funny one."

"I'd never be able to remember the punch line." She nervously glanced down at her lap and then at her shoes and then outside. The sky had changed from an ominous gray to a shimmering white that held promising patches of blue. Her gaze softened and she drifted into private thoughts again, comparing her dreams of Eric to the real man.

"Why the smile?" Eric asked, curious about the transformation he had just witnessed.

"Oh . . . I was just thinking." As always, she was hesitant to reveal too much of herself.

"About?" he prodded.

She glanced over to him, trying to judge how he would react if she were to tell him the truth. She decided to take a chance. "Last night when you found me asleep on the couch . . ."

"Uh-huh."

"I was in the middle of a dream."

He had guessed as much.

"You were in that dream."

He had guessed that, too, but he liked having her tell him. "And?"

"I was just thinking how different this . . . how different today is from my dream."

"Tell me about it."

"I'd rather not."

"Why?"

"It would embarrass me."

"Then how about if I tell you my dream first?"

She eyed him suspiciously.

Eric reached over and tugged on her wrist until her hand was free from beneath her leg. He held it while he talked, as if needing the contact. "Every dream that we're in together is a little different than the last, but the time and place are always the same. We are alone on the ocean on the deck of a sailboat, and it's nearing sunset. . . ." His voice grew wistful. "You're wearing white shorts and a loose top, and your skin is tanned to a golden bronze color that glows in the lingering sunlight. I finish working on the sails, and you come over to me. . . ." What came next was too intimate to share.

"And?" she softly prodded.

He could feel a warmth spreading through him. "And you put your arms around me . . . your body tastes salty. . . ."

When he hesitated again, Janet haltingly told him about her own dream, which with minor variations was always the same. She described the filmy white dress, cut low in the front and with a full skirt that caught in the lightest breeze and gently caressed her legs. He was dressed in a tuxedo, and they were in each other's arms, dancing to soft music.

Then they were alone, standing on a balcony overlooking the ocean, sharing a glass of wine. They stared longingly into each other's eyes, their desire heightened by purposely not touching.

Later they walked along a beach, silhouetted by a glorious orange-and-pink sunset. Eric's tie hung loose, and the top three buttons of his shirt were undone, revealing a light matting of dark hair. His pants were rolled up to midcalf, and he carried his jacket flung over his shoulder, hooked on two fingers. Janet walked beside him, her stockings in his coat pocket, her heels dangling by their straps from one hand, her other hand clasping Eric's. Then they turned to gaze at each other, communicating their growing need without exchanging a word.

Soon they started walking again, continuing until they reached a sheltered area where cypress grew close to the softly lapping surf. Eric laid his jacket and her shoes on the now moon-bathed sand and reached for her, drawing her into his arms. . . .

Too embarrassed to go on, Janet's voice faded to a whisper and then disappeared altogether.

Eric smiled knowingly as he turned off the main road onto a narrower country lane flanked by vineyards. He gave her hand a gentle squeeze. "When we come back here next year, you won't recognize these fields," he said, gracefully changing the subject. With no branches growing along the wires strung over the gnarled plants and leaves, the fields looked barren. Only twisted stumps were left behind, a reminder of the glorious richness that would return the next spring.

Janet felt a moment of panic. Everything was happening so fast between them. Where were they going? What were they doing? What kind of relationship were they establishing between them today? She looked at Eric. The overwhelming hunger that controlled her refused to recognize the possibility that they might be making a horrible mistake.

"Here we are."

They had stopped in front of a Queen Anne style, two-story house that looked out over the valley with a regal air of authority. Steep gables and a corner turret capped the ornamental shingle work on the second story, and a wide porch ran three-quarters of the way along the front of the first story. The grounds surrounding the house were meticulously tended, and the flower beds were filled with masses of fall color. "What do you mean, cabin?" she gasped, looking around her at what any normal person would have called a mansion.

"I guess 'summer home' would probably be a better description," he answered, reaching for the car handle, oblivious to her stunned reaction to the opulence of a home he had always taken for granted.

"Who takes care of this place?" She joined him on the path that led to the front door.

"A couple who live in that brown-and-white house we passed on the way up. They've been here for as long as I can remember."

After climbing the front steps up to the porch, Janet walked over to the railing. Her gaze swept the acres of vineyards. "I suppose all this land is yours, too?"

Eric joined her. "Actually, it belongs to my grandparents. A long time ago my grandfather had a yearning to have his own winery. He changed his mind when he discovered he couldn't grow the quality of grapes here that he needed to produce the valley's best wine, and since he refused to settle for anything less, he gave up the project. Still, he couldn't quite bring himself to sell the place, but he couldn't let such choice land lay fallow, either. So he leases it out." He stuck his hands in his pockets. "Would you like me to show you around the place?"

She gave him a slow smile. "Could it wait until later?"

"It could even wait for another time." He slipped his arm around her waist and drew her near.

Running her hands down his jacket lapels, she looked up into his eyes. "However, I wouldn't mind seeing the inside."

He unlocked the front door, and they went in. Janet was delighted to see that the interior held a warm and welcoming mixture of old and new furniture and was not—as she feared it might be—a showplace for precious antiques that demanded more attention than the guests.

Noticing what he was afraid were second thoughts in her eyes, Eric took her into his arms again. "You don't have to go through with this, you know," he told her.

"I know," she answered, the last of her reservations melting under the warmth of his concern.

He reached for her hand and silently led her up the spiral staircase to the room that had been his since he was a child. A double bed, covered by a navy-blue goose down comforter, faced a pair of dormer windows that overlooked the valley. In the far corner a worn-out first baseman's glove hung from a baseball bat. On the wall was a poster of a ship in full sail. Janet liked the idea that someone's sentimentality had dictated leaving touches of Eric's childhood in the room. She walked over to the window and pulled the sheer curtain to the side. Shafts of sunlight had broken through the clouds to form brilliant circles of green on the valley floor.

Eric shrugged out of his jacket and tossed it on the dresser before he went over to stand behind her. His arms encircled her waist. Slowly they moved up her sides until they were touching the fullness of her breasts. Janet sighed and pressed herself against him, resting the back of her head on the side of his neck. With deft fingers he released the tiny pearl buttons that ran down the front of her sweater. Pulling the soft knit aside, he unclasped her bra and cupped her breasts, letting them fill his hands.

Janet leaned into him, feeling the tension in his muscles as he responded to her pressure. She turned her head to meet his questing mouth and was lost in the unleashed hunger of his kiss. Never had she been swept so completely into the uncompromising world of passion.

Eric removed his own clothing and took her over to stand beside the bed. Slowly, as if time were a gift to be spent lavishly, he finished undressing her. When everything was gone but the wisp of silky material that hugged her hips, he caught her to him, reveling in the singular pleasure of her nearly naked body against his own. Moving his hands the length of her back, he slipped them beneath the elastic of her panties and cupped her buttocks. He trailed kisses down her neck and across her shoulder, then slowly dropped to his knees as his lips moved lower.

Janet's eyes closed. Her breath caught in her throat. She sighed. Her fingers entwined in his hair as she moved to accept his kisses. She felt silk material caress her thighs, to be replaced briefly by the silken touch of Eric's lips. Then she felt herself being lifted and placed on the bed.

When he lay down beside her, Eric's hands again paid homage to the gentle swells and curves of her body as he sought to imprint the feel, the texture, the rhythm of her response to him on his mind. The journey grew progressively more intimate . . . and then he sought yet new understanding of her with the sensitive touch of his mouth.

He pressed his lips to the base of her throat and felt the demanding beat of her pulse. With the tip of his tongue he traced a thin, moist line to her breast. Gently he touched the nipple with his lips, feeling a sweet satisfaction when it hardened in response to his caress. He took the peak into his mouth and pressed his face against the yielding, erotic flesh. She softly moaned and caught the back of his head to draw him closer.

His hand left her waist, paused to cup her hip, then moved on to the flatness of her stomach. She caught her breath as he moved lower, his fingers fanning out to encompass the triangle of curling hair before dipping lower still to unerringly find the place where she ached to be touched.

Gently, lovingly, expertly he stroked her, and with all that had gone before, she felt herself nearing climax. She caught his hand and stilled him. "Not yet," she sighed, wanting him to take that final journey with her.

He stared at her, looking deeply into her eyes. Slowly his mouth curved into a compelling sensual smile. "This time I'm in charge," he told her, his voice low and husky as he brushed her hand away. Purposely he separated her thighs and moved lower, trailing moist kisses down her abdomen. When he intimately touched her again, it was his tongue that did the stroking...coaxing, leading, taunting, until she was brought to a shattering peak of excitement unlike any she had known before. Wave after wave of intense release swept over her until she thought it would never stop.

Eric held himself suspended over her, watching, relishing the sight of the pleasure he had given her. Slowly she reached up and held the sides of his face with her hands. Her expression told him the intimacy they had shared had been special, not given or taken lightly. He was profoundly pleased by the message, but not suprised. She had been wonderfully expressive.

Janet's hands left his face and began a lingering journey through the light matting of hair on his chest, following the narrowing trail until the texture changed, as well as her objective. Eric caught his breath as she intimately touched and then encircled him, alternately pressing and releasing him. He moved against her hand, the tension in him growing, the need for release becoming a sweet agony.

Finally, with insistent urging, she brought him to her, wrapping her legs around his waist. With a swift, sure thrust he entered her, stealing her breath with the intensity of his need. But still he held off, waiting for her, whispering words of encouragement, touching, kissing, erotically moving against her until he heard the soft moan, the hesitant sigh, and felt her grow tense beneath him, telling him she was ready to accompany him on the final journey. As was all that had gone before, the climax to their lovemaking was explosive, leaving them physically and emotionally exhausted.

Afterward Eric held her, cradling her against his side, whispering words of love as he gently touched her. Slowly their worlds righted themselves again. And as they did, thoughts and feelings swirled around Janet in an emotional storm. Doubts about what they had just done crashed down around her. She turned from Eric, rolling over onto her side.

"What is it?" he asked, touching her arm and turning her back to face him.

"I can't tell you—" She sighed. "I don't know myself." But she did. She was afraid of what was happening to her. The way Eric had made love to her had made her realize that what they had started today was more than she could handle. Slowly, like petals being stripped from a rose, with each kiss, with each sigh, she felt herself relinquishing by minute increments complete control of her own destiny.

"Janet, don't close me out." Frantically he sought to reach her, to pull her back from the place she had gone. When she hesitated, he sought his answer in the depths of her eyes. He was stunned when what he found was fear. "What have I done to deserve you being afraid of me?" he demanded.

"Nothing," she softly cried. "It isn't you—it's me. I can't give you what you want, Eric."

"You can't love me? Why not?"

"How can I make you understand? It isn't that I don't want to love you, it's that I don't have the time."

Eric rolled onto his back and stared up at the ceiling. "I'm not sure you could ever make me understand something like that, Janet." As he lay there anger welled up inside him. "Tell me—how much time does it take to love someone? How many hours a day could you be compelled to spend away from your regular routine?"

His questions were met by silence.

8

WITHOUT THEIR PASSION to warm them, the room soon grew cold. Eric sat up to gather the comforter over them. Janet reached for her sweater as if to start getting dressed.

"Not yet," he said, grasping her elbow and pulling her back down beside him. "We still have some talking to do."

"Don't you think it would be better if we did our talking somewhere else . . . and with our clothes on?"

"I can't think of another place I'd rather be than right here, with you dressed precisely the way you are now." He tucked a puff of down under her chin. "Now give—what in hell is this nonsense about not loving me because you don't have the time?"

"Remember when we were in your office and you asked me to go out with you?"

He smiled. "And you said you would, a week from Friday."

In spite of herself, a return smile twitched at the corner of Janet's mouth. It gave her a peculiar pleasure to realize he remembered that day so well. "Just in case you haven't been able to figure it out by now, that was one of my good weeks. I've gone as long as a month without enough time off for a quick date. How am I ever supposed to work having an affair with you into my schedule?" Saying the words aloud made her heart sink.

He was at a loss for a reply. There were several possible solutions that came to mind, but he knew without suggesting them what her answer would be. She was far too independent to accept financial help from him at this point in their relationship. On that possibility, he would have to bide his time. "Then I guess there'll just have to be some months when we'll only get to see each other once."

Janet eyed him, looking for signs of prevarication. "You can't be serious."

"I didn't say I would like the arrangement. But it seems I have no choice."

She wiggled farther down under the comforter. "You're giving in far too easily."

"Meaning you don't trust me?"

"Now you're acting just like a lawyer—trying to win your point by putting me on the defensive."

In spite of the skepticism in her words, he felt her physically relaxing and knew that she was slowly coming around to believing him. He felt a twinge of guilt for being less than honest with her, but since it was a matter of whether he would see her again, he would have done far worse. "I told you once that I'd been waiting a long time for you, Janet," he said, unmistakable determination in his voice. "Did you think I'd give up so easily?"

She was tired of fighting a battle she really wanted to lose. Besides, what had he left her to argue about? But in spite of her attempt to adopt a Pollyanna attitude, somewhere in the back of her mind a warning voice sounded, telling her they were fooling themselves to think the arrangement she proposed could ever work out for them. It was beyond reason to stretch anyone's patience as thin as Eric's would be by the time he'd waited the almost three years it would take her to finish school. But the day was too beautiful and being with him too glorious for her to dwell on the negative.

She pulled the comforter over her head and moved to his side. Nuzzling her face against the light matting of hair on his chest, she found his nipple and made a circle around it with her tongue. She smiled in satisfaction when she heard his sharp intake of breath. Before Eric could respond further, she grabbed his arm and covered it with nibbling bites.

He joined her under the covers. "By any chance would these teeth marks on my arm mean you're hungry?"

"Only if there's something besides what's in the car to eat around here."

"And I suppose you would have me brave the cold waiting for me down in the kitchen to find out."

She blinked. "Why. . . how sweet of you to offer."

He caught her to him and buried his face between her breasts. *God, she felt so good.* It wasn't just her nakedness that made him feel so good or the beautiful symmetry of her body or the way she smelled as nice as all the summer days he had ever known rolled into one, it wasn't even the way she looked at him when they were making love; it was the special joy of finally having her, at last, really with him. He felt like returning to San Francisco and standing atop the Transamerica Building and shouting that he had been right to wait for her and not settle for less. He had been vindicated. She was everything he had known she would be.

He gave her a lusty kiss and jumped out of bed. "Keep my side warm for me. I'll be right back."

Janet peeked at him from behind the covers. "Right. I'll just lie here spread-eagled until you get back."

He gave her a wicked grin. "If you keep talking like that, I'll never leave." He slipped into his jeans and pulled on his shirt before blowing her a goodbye kiss.

When he was gone, her confidence began to abandon her. To pass the time while she waited for him to return, she tried to calculate the minimum number of hours she would have to work in November to pay the bills and still set some money aside for Christmas. Usually her only variable each month was the amount of time she spent on homework. And to let that slide now was unthinkable. It wouldn't make much sense for her to work as hard as she did to pay her tuition if she wasn't going to keep her grades up. The more she thought about the impossibility of her and Eric being together, the more depressed she became. By the time he returned, she had trouble dredging up a smile.

He stood by the door, tray in hand, staring at her. "I see you've been thinking while I was gone," he said with a heavy sigh. He put the tray on the nightstand, sat on the edge of the bed and took her hand in his. "The only way this is ever going to work is if we agree we have to take things one day at a time." He absently caressed her palm with his thumb. "Instead of thinking how bad next week or next month is going to be, why don't we concentrate on how much we can be together during the upcoming holidays or at the semester break when you'll have more free time."

She sat up, pulled her knees to her chest and propped her chin on her knees. "If you're trying to cheer me up, you just picked a bum way to do it. Holidays and semester breaks are the periods I have the least amount of time off. Without classes or homework to slow me down, I can work both jobs every day. It's the only way I can earn enough to pay the next semester's tuition"

For the first time, Eric felt a stab of doubt. "What about a loan?" he said softly.

"I've already gone that route." She laughed humorlessly. "As it stands now, I'll probably be in my forties before I've finished paying for my education."

"I wasn't talking about a government loan." He was testing her to see how far she would let him go in his offer to help.

Her eyes flew open, filled with anger. "Are you suggesting what I think you're suggesting?"

"Why not?" he asked evenly, reasonably.

Now her eyes narrowed. "I *knew* you wouldn't understand." She threw back the covers and started to get out of bed.

Eric lunged for her, pinning her beneath him. "Would you please get it through your head that I'm not going to let you make a grand exit until we have things cleared up between us?"

"Let go of me."

"Absolutely not."

His answer momentarily stunned her. "What do you mean, absolutely not?" She couldn't remember the last time she had told someone to do something and had been so summarily refused. Wheedled and cajoled into changing her mind, maybe, but never categorically refused.

"What I mean is that if it takes until next week, you and I will stay exactly as we are until you tell me you sincerely believe things will work out between us."

For long seconds she stared at him. "I think things will work out for us," she finally said, her jaw tight in frustration at being so completely physically overpowered.

"Now why do you suppose it is that I don't think you really mean what you just said?"

"I can't imagine." She tried wiggling out from beneath him. "I can't breathe," she complained.

He raised himself slightly. "Why is the idea of accepting a loan from me so reprehensible?"

They were so different. The worlds they inhabited were so far apart. How could she ever make him understand someone like herself? "I know it will be hard for someone like you, but try for a couple of minutes to put yourself in my place. Let's say you were in a hand-to-mouth situation and through a weird set of circumstances you wound up with a girlfriend who was so rich that she had trouble talking around the silver spoon stuck in her mouth." An impish twinkle flashed from her eyes. "Now we're not talking your average well-to-do rich lady, mind you; we're talking so rich that the poor kid doesn't know a cabin from a mansion."

"I think I've got the picture; you can get on with it now."

"Since this girl has obviously been raised with the attitude that if you want something, you buy it, it only seems reasonable to her to assume the philosophy would work when it came to buying her boyfriend's time. There's one major problem—the boyfriend doesn't happen to like the feeling that he's being bought."

"Is that how Robert felt when you were putting him through school?"

"It's not the same thing at all."

"Why not?"

"Because Robert and I were married."

Gut instinct told him to lead with his chin. "Then marry me."

His words hurt her more than she had ever suspected words could hurt. Not only hadn't he been listening to her, but he thought everything she had been trying to tell him was a joke. Tears of anger and frustration and pain welled up in her eyes. "How can you be so—" A sob caught in her throat, and she couldn't finish.

"I take it that means no?" He was completely confused by her reaction to his sincere proposal.

"Damn you!"

The confusion multiplied tenfold. "For asking you to marry me?"

"For not taking me seriously."

He rolled onto his side, taking her with him. She struggled a moment and then lay still in his arms. "What do you say we go back to square one and try this all over again? I won't offer to loan you any money, and you won't swear at me for asking you to marry me."

Something fragile had been broken between them, and fearing it might be a permanent break, Janet was just as anxious to try to mend it as he was. "Eric...we're so completely different that our life-styles don't even have a nodding acquaintance." She sought a better way to explain. "I feel like we're characters out of that song, *The Cowboy and the Lady*. Only it's me who's the cowboy."

He gave her a crooked grin. "And I suppose that means I'm the lady?"

She tilted her chin up so that she could look him directly in the eyes. "Do you have any idea what it is I'm trying to say?"

He became serious again. "I can't help being born rich, Janet, anymore than you can help being who you are. And I'm afraid someone would have me locked up if I tried to give my money away." He brushed a curl from her temple. "Somehow I never figured you for the prejudiced type."

"I'm not," she said indignantly.

"Well, then, recognize the fact that rich people need love, too, even if it happens to come from struggling students."

It wasn't just the money that bothered her, it was the miles between them on the social scale. The one time she had gone to the opera, she had hated it; and the food she liked all leaned toward the steak and potato variety. "My father always told me I'd wind up stumbling over my pride someday. I guess he knew what he was talking about."

He kissed the end of her nose. "I wouldn't change a thing about you—I love you just the way you are."

She grinned. "I feel like a contestant on *Name that Tune*."

"Well, let's play later. Right now I want to eat." He sat up and reached for the tray. On it were two bowls of fruit cocktail, a plate of dark brown chocolate chip cookies and two glasses of tomato juice.

Janet laughed aloud at the conglomeration. "I can't believe it; I'm so hungry that this actually looks good."

"It was either this or green beans and candied yams. That was all I could find in the cupboard."

"You did a wonderful job."

They leaned against the headboard. The tray rested on Eric's lap. He handed her a bowl and a spoon. "Wait," she commanded when she saw him start to take a bite. "Did you use the whole can?"

"Yes."

"Let me see your bowl."

Puzzled, he obliged, handing it over for her inspection. She moved some chunks of peaches with her spoon and looked under a pear before returning to her own bowl of fruit. He waited until it became obvious she had no intention of offering an explanation. "Did I pass?"

She purposely looked at him, letting her gaze linger on his thighs and the wedge of bare skin where his shirt hung open. When she had finished, she winked. "And so did the fruit cocktail."

How easily she could excite him. "I assume you're going to tell me what this is all about?"

She nodded but continued to eat. Finally she stopped long enough to explain. "When I was a kid, someone once told me there were supposed to be exactly four half cherries in every can of fruit cocktail. Ever since then, I have been unable to eat the stuff without checking it out first."

"And?"

"It's running about ninety-five percent so far." Finishing the last bite of her fruit, she reached for a cookie.

Eric was enchanted. He had been raised in a family that had the same whimsical way of looking at life. When he'd been growing up, August wasn't just another summer month, it was a magical time of staying up all night to watch shooting stars. And long after he and Susan had stopped believing in Santa Claus, on every Christmas eve his mother had still left carrots by the fireplace for the reindeer. It had only been a few years ago that he had learned it was his father who had crept down the stairs every Christmas morning to nibble on the carrots.

He waited for Janet to finish her cookie. "What do you think?"

"About how they look or how they taste?"

"Either—both."

She picked up another cookie and studied it. "They look like hockey pucks, but they taste great. What did you do to them?"

"You mean why are they so dark?" When she nodded, he told her. "I mixed cocoa in with the flour."

"Clever idea. It gives them a double chocolate taste."

"Thanks," he said with no attempt at modesty. "I've been working hard to improve my cooking lately, and not many people have noticed."

"For any special reasons?" She took another bite. "Improving your cooking, I mean, not the no one noticing part."

He laughed. "Besides self-defense?"

"I'm surprised you don't have someone who does your cooking for you."

"What would I ever do with a cook on *The Promise*?" He twisted around to put the now empty tray back on the nightstand.

Here we go again, she thought. There were times when she felt they were speaking different languages. "Just what is it with you and this promising business you're always talking about?"

He turned back around to look at her, an eyebrow raised in question. "What did you have in mind?" But his thoughts weren't on her answer—they were on the incredible fact that she was actually in his bed, sitting there beside him with nothing on but a blanket. She had pulled the comforter up to her chest when she sat up to eat, leaving her shoulders and the creamy skin above her breasts bare—an enticement that destroyed every other thought.

He bent over and touched the gentle swelling that rose above the blanket with his tongue, capturing a cookie crumb. Warming to his task, he found another and then nudged the blanket lower with his chin as if to search for more. "We have to be careful these don't wind up in the bed," he murmured.

"I understand," she breathed, letting the delicious feel of his touch spread all over her and warm her like sunshine after a week of rain.

Leisurely he moved the blanket lower, paying careful attention to the newly exposed skin, luxuriating in her anticipatory sighs. When he had completely uncovered her breasts, he took first one and then the other nipple into his mouth, caressing them to responsive peaks. Slowly he traced a moist line of fleeting kisses down to her navel. As he started to move lower, Janet reached out to stop him.

"I . . . uh . . ." She tried to swallow, her mouth suddenly gone dry. "I don't think . . ." Her words died when he gave her a devastatingly intimate smile that made her ache for the pleasure his kisses had promised.

"Good," he said, his voice husky with desire, "I don't want you to think—I want you to feel." His hand slid down her hip and across the flat of her belly to her inner thighs. When he felt her resist, he gently coaxed, "Let go, Janet. Let me love you in every way I know how. Let me give myself to you in every way that I can."

Subconsciously she responded to his words and stopped fighting him. Unerringly he found the place that ached to be touched, and she took the first step on a sensuous one-way journey.

SEVERAL HOURS LATER, they were still in bed. It was
dark outside when finally they broke down and acknowledged that it was time to talk about returning to
San Francisco. They had spent those idyllic hours in the
world of lovers, one that had been finely focused on
only themselves. Slowly they were coming to know
each other, discovering birthmarks and scars and telling birthdays and secrets. The one thing they purposely avoided talking about was when and where they
would see each other again. Still, the unanswered
question persisted, an open wound neither knew how
to heal.

It wasn't until they were back at Eric's house in San
Francisco that anything was said. Janet had walked
around the car to get in the driver's side, and Eric had
taken her into his arms to kiss her good-night. "I told
myself I wouldn't ask," he said, his cheek buried in the
softness of her hair, "but is there a chance I could see
you tomorrow?" He was anxious to show her *The
Promise*. He was anxious to make love to her again. He
was anxious to spend another day telling her of his
love....

Her heart sank. It was beginning already. "Amy and
Brian will be back tomorrow."

"Amy and Brian?" Who in hell were Amy and Brian?

"Carol's kids." Surely she had told him how she
earned her room and board.

"Who's Carol?"

Obviously she hadn't. As succinctly as possible, she
told him about Amy and Brian and Carol.

For the first time, Eric felt a sense of despair creep into
his conviction that they could work things out. He had
figured their one ace in the hole would be his ability to
take off an occasional afternoon so they could meet for

a few hours after her classes. Her news about living with someone and baby-sitting for them destroyed that possibility. Finally he understood what she had been trying to tell him. "Then I guess you'll call me when you can work something out?" Despite his attempts to hide it, a note of deep frustration crept into his voice.

"Eric . . . I tried to tell you."

"I know you did."

"Surely you don't think this is any easier on me?"

Responding to her defensive tone, he pulled her close. "No, my beautiful, stubborn Janet, I don't think you will sleep any easier at night than I will." Somehow, some way, he was going to have to convince her to let him help.

Her fight disappeared as quickly as it had come, and she relaxed in his arms. "Oh, Eric . . . what if we wind up hating each other?"

He cupped her chin in his hand and forced her to look at him. "Do you honestly think that's possible?"

"You forget, I've been this route before. Only with Robert, what we had died such a slow uncomplaining death that we were shocked to find it gone."

He lowered his lips to hers and gave her a kiss that demanded she recognize the special thing that was happening between them, and it was unlike anything that had ever happened to either of them before. "Stay with me tonight," he said, suddenly unwilling to let her go now that he knew it might be weeks before they had any real time to spend together again.

She was sorely tempted, not only to stay that night, but the next and the next. "I can't," she sighed. "Amy fixes me breakfast on Sunday mornings. How would I ever explain . . ."

As much as he wanted her to stay, he liked the idea that she felt an obligation to a six-year-old girl who thought it a special treat to fix her friend breakfast. Obviously Janet was a person who cared for children.

"Come on." He lightly kissed her forehead and reached for the car door. "It's already later than I think it's safe for you to be driving home alone."

She suppressed a smile. Eric was going to take some getting used to. For over three years she had been the sole decision maker in every aspect of her life. Having another opinion to deal with might prove difficult at times. "I thought we went through this once already," she gently scolded. "But if you like, I'll call you when I get home to let you know I arrived safe and sound and in one piece."

"That's a great idea. Do you have this number?"

She had only been kidding. "Are you serious?"

"Weren't you?"

"Sure...yeah, I guess I was." She didn't have the heart to tell him differently. She dug a piece of paper and a pen out of her purse and wrote down the number.

When she was inside the car and had her seat belt in place, Eric bent down and gave her a kiss that she felt all the way down to her toes. "You sure know how to make it hard to leave," she breathed.

"I don't want you to forget me."

"Fat chance."

He stood in the driveway, watching until her taillights disappeared around the corner before picking up the picnic basket, opening the front door and going inside. He put the basket in the kitchen, then went into the study to pour himself a brandy. Purposely not turning on the lights, he wandered over to the window to watch the late-night traffic on the bridge. A frustration more profound than any he had ever known before gripped his stomach. He had thought himself clever to give in so easily to her refusal to accept his help, thinking there would be plenty of opportunity to work on her. Now he found he was in a catch-22 situation—without the time off she would have if she let him help her financially, he would never get the chance to talk her into letting him help her.

For once the breathtaking beauty before him failed to bring him peace, and he wandered away from the window as depressed as when he arrived.

9

JANET LOOKED UP from her cornflakes to see Carol staring at her. She had lived with Carol long enough to know she had not fooled her into thinking today was like any other day. But it wasn't until the dishes were being cleared that something was said.

"Why do you look like the cat that's been in the cream?"

Stopping to pop the last bite of her blueberry muffin into her mouth, Janet feigned a look of innocence. "You're imagining things."

Carol stepped closer and lowered her voice so that the children wouldn't hear. "I know that special glow, my friend, and it only comes from one source. Now give—what have you been doing while I was gone?"

From anyone else the question would have smacked of prying; from Carol, Janet knew it was genuine caring. "I took your advice and went out with Eric Stewart."

"And?"

"And we had a good time."

"Judging from the way you look this morning, I would say that's a monumental understatement if I ever heard one."

Janet grinned. "All right—we had a wonderful time." She opened the dishwasher and started stacking the breakfast dishes while Carol put the milk and cereal away. This was their Sunday morning tradition. Amy cooked, and they cleaned up after her.

"So now what?"

"That's precisely what I've been asking myself all morning."

Standing on her toes to shove the cereal box into the overhead cupboard, Carol grimaced. "Seems to me you're caught between a rock and a hard place, with Eric on one side and school on the other. You'll never be able to do justice to one without the other suffering."

"We talked about that yesterday, and Eric was very understanding."

"Uh-huh, but for how long? I assume this guy is human."

"What is this, some weird kind of support?"

"If you don't look at things realistically, they'll never work out." She grabbed the dishcloth and started to wipe down the countertops, cleaning a wide trail of blueberry-muffin batter. "Why don't we take a few minutes to sit down this morning and see if we can't readjust our schedules so you can have some time off that will coordinate with his?"

Janet felt a tightness behind her eyes that meant they were about to fill with tears. Along with the good feelings left over from the day before were grave doubts about the speed at which everything was happening. She and Eric desperately needed time together to discover if the way they felt about each other was real. It was just like Carol to offer her that time. "How did I ever deserve a friend like you?"

Carol came over to put her arms around Janet. "By being a wonderful friend to me. I'm only giving back what I get."

After the kitchen was clean, they took paper and pencil and sat down with second cups of coffee in the living room. They made a chart listing the seven days of the week and all the waking hours. When they had finished filling it in with the demands on Janet's time that could not be readily changed, they started to work on the open hours. Time she had used between classes to visit with friends, no matter how brief, would now be used for studying. Janet felt a twinge of sadness, knowing there would be no more crazy conversations or discussions of world affairs with Earthquake and his roommate. And Casey would have to find someone else to tell about her latest fling. But she promised herself that somehow she wouldn't let either friendship die for lack of attention. The other gatherings, mostly spontaneous, when groups of students would leave a lecture and continue discussing something interesting that had been brought up in class that day, would just have to be foregone.

In the end, Janet was pleasantly surprised. They had worked it out so that every Sunday when she wasn't chauffeuring clients to a Forty-niners football game at Candlestick Park, she could have free to spend with Eric. And even on the days she did drive, she would have the evenings off. Sunday morning breakfasts with Amy would be moved to Saturdays, and Carol would talk the other members of the string quartet she usually practiced with on Sunday afternoons into moving their meetings to Wednesday nights. All of which meant she would be able to see Eric for a full day again the Sunday after next.

"Now all you have to do is make sure you stay healthy, and everything will work out fine," Carol said, taking the chart they had made into the kitchen and pinning it up on the cork bulletin board.

Janet followed her in with the coffee cups. While she was putting them into the dishwasher, the phone rang. Carol answered, then held out the receiver. "It's for you—Earthquake."

For an instant, thinking it might be Eric, Janet's heart had picked up its rhythm. She had a burgeoning need to hear his voice and to tell him the good news. "What's up?" she said, her tone reflecting her inner happiness.

"I just called to remind you about the protest."

Her mind rapidly sorted through bits and pieces of information seeking out one about a protest. "Give me a bigger hint."

"I knew it. You forgot, didn't you?"

"Come on, Earthquake . . . just one tiny little clue."

"Lawrence Livermore Laboratory? Any bells ringing?"

They were—all too loudly. The last time she had distributed antinuclear pamphlets with him, she had faithfully promised to be a part of the upcoming demonstration. "When is it?"

"In two weeks."

She closed her eyes and leaned her head against the wall. "On a Sunday?" She didn't have to ask, she already knew.

"So you did remember. I'm proud of you."

"No . . . I didn't. It was just a lucky guess."

"You don't sound too excited. Is something wrong?"

She tried to say the words that would get her out of going but couldn't. She recalled all too vividly when she had promised to go with him. He had been ecstatic. *Oh, Eric, please understand when I tell you that it will be four weeks instead of two before we can spend the day together again.* "Of course there's nothing wrong, Earthquake. I'm just a little tired."

"Late night, huh?"

"Yeah." She ran her hand through her hair. "Do you want me to drive?"

"As long as it's not raining, it might be better if we took my motorcycle. That way if we get arrested, it will be easier for someone to get it to the jail. They can just throw it in the back of a pickup."

Now everything came back to her, hitting her like an avalanche. The discussions they had had, between classes and during their walks, about being dedicated enough to a cause to go to jail for it echoed tauntingly in her mind. With a sinking feeling she remembered giving her wholehearted endorsement to the project, never thinking it would really come to pass. It wasn't that she didn't passionately believe Carl Sagen was right when he said any nuclear conflict meant total annihilation, or that using nuclear power for energy was tantamount to playing Russian roulette with the environment, it just wasn't a good time for her to prove how much she cared. Her reasoning made her feel so guilty that any thought of backing out became impossible. "What time do you want me to be ready?" she sighed.

"I'll pick you up at three-thirty."

"In the morning?" she screeched.

"It's a surprise attack. The media isn't even being notified until we're already there."

Spending an hour and a half on the back of a motorcycle in the dead of winter in the dead of the night had about as much appeal as the food on one of Eric's picnic lunches. "Don't be disappointed if I'm not my usual radiant self that morning."

He laughed. "No problem. Conversation's a little tough on a bike, anyway."

They talked awhile longer about the upcoming biology midterm before saying goodbye and hanging up. When Janet turned around, she saw Carol looking at her, her hands on her hips, a frown on her face.

"Did I hear what I thought I heard?" she said.

Janet shrugged helplessly. "What could I do? I promised."

"You should have told him about Eric. I'm sure he would have understood."

"Carol, Earthquake is still young enough to think something like this protest can really make a difference. He needs gung ho support, not apathy. Who knows, maybe someday he will be the one who gains a position powerful enough to save us all from this insanity. Think how wrong it would be for me to discourage him now."

Carol made a face and rolled her eyes. "I can't believe I'm hearing this."

"Neither can I. I'm going to my room now to try to get some studying done before you have to leave. Let me know when you're ready." She reached up to close a cupboard on her way out, almost tripping on a Transformer that Brian had left in the doorway. "Sorry," she absently mumbled to the car-robot as she made her way down the hallway.

An hour later she had read her biology notes twice but couldn't remember a word. It was no good. She had to call Eric and explain about Earthquake. She picked up the phone and made the call; he answered on the first ring as if he'd been waiting for her.

"And here I thought it was going to be an ordinary morning," he said, his voice a verbal caress.

"Don't be nice to me," she groaned. "You'll only make me feel worse."

He had been sitting at his desk, gathering up the merger papers he had been going over that morning, when her phone call came. At the tone in her voice he shoved the papers aside and gave her his full attention. "What's wrong, Janet?"

"I have good news and bad news. Which do you want first?"

"The good."

"Carol and I spent the morning juggling my schedule, and I now have every Sunday off that there isn't a home game for the Forty-niners."

"And the bad?" he asked warily.

"Except for a few hours next Sunday evening, I won't be able to see you again for three weeks."

"I don't understand."

She started to tell him about Earthquake but decided it was easier simply to say she had made previous commitments.

There was a long pause. "I'm afraid next Sunday's out of the question, too. I'm catching a plane for Detroit that afternoon."

"Oh...I see." At no time in her thinking had she considered that they might have to work around his schedule, too.

"You don't have even a couple of hours during the middle of the week? I could rent a car and meet you someplace."

"I have some time between classes."

"There's no way I could leave the office this next week. My calendar is full." Frustration became a tangible barrier between them. It was one thing for two people to suffer a separation after their relationship had

had time to grow and for bonds to develop that would hold them together; it was something else entirely when that relationship had so recently been formed and was necessarily as fragile as are all newborn things. "Janet . . ." He said her name with all the love that welled inside him. "Don't lose heart. We'll find a way."

They were simple words, but they were the right words. Little by little, she was coming to realize how special Eric was and how much he was worth the sacrifices she might have to make to see him. To save her the added expense of long-distance phone bills, he told her he would do the calling from then on. They set up days and times and unwillingly said goodbye. Afterward, Janet found it far easier to concentrate and was in a terrific mood when it came time for her to take Brian and Amy to the park.

THE FOLLOWING WEEK Eric called three times but only found Janet home once. For all the lip service he had paid to the need for patience, he discovered his patience was wearing impossibly thin. It was all he could do to hide it from Janet when he called early the next Sunday morning to tell her goodbye before he left for Detroit. Though he wouldn't be leaving for the airport for several hours, she had to be in Daly City to pick up a customer and take him and his party to the football game, which necessitated the early call.

"When will you be back?" she asked, sitting on the corner of the bed, trying to put her makeup on while looking into a mirror she held balanced on her lap.

"Wednesday or possibly Thursday."

"I'll miss you."

He absently massaged his temple. "I'd be a little more excited about that if you wouldn't also be missing me if I were staying right here in town."

How could she ever have thought this arrangement would work? Slowly, inexorably she felt herself being backed into a corner. "I've been thinking about next semester. If I could arrange my classes so that I only went on Tuesdays and Thursdays, we'd have another day to be together."

"And if you'd stop being so stubborn and let me help you out just a little, we'd have another day right now. Dammit, Janet, I'm not talking about taking over your life or trying to tie you to me in any way, I just want to give you a helping hand so we can be together more often." He was growing more and more convinced that doing things her way would eventually drive a wedge between them that they'd never be able to surmount.

"Buying me is what you're talking about. I don't care how you phrase it, Eric, it boils down to the same thing." She glanced over to the clock on the night-stand. She had less than ten minutes to finish dressing and get on the road. "Call me when you get back. We'll finish this then."

Why was he fighting with her when what he wanted more than anything else was to take her in his arms and tell her how much he loved her. "Can you stop by the office Thursday before you go to Coachman's?"

She would be delivering balloons on Thursday, which meant she'd have to show up at his office in costume again. Parading around in baggy pants and greasepaint in front of his friends and colleagues was the last thing she wanted to do. "I'll try, but I can't promise. If my last delivery is across town, I'd never be able to make it to your office and then all the way over to Coachman's on time." She looked at the clock again. Now she only had five minutes. She stood and shrugged out of her bathrobe. "I have to go now, Eric."

He resigned himself to waiting another five days to put his case before her one more time. He was becoming a little discouraged. Instead of the signs he had been watching for, that he was breaking down her resistance, she seemed to be more determined than ever to refuse his help. "Drive carefully." An ache gnawed at his insides.

"I always do." *Why now*, she wanted to scream. What screwy toss of the dice had brought Eric Stewart into her life at precisely the wrong time? When she hung up she was struck by a feeling of incredible emptiness. But, as usual, there wasn't time to dwell on how miserable she felt. Even with no tie-ups on the freeway, she was already going to be late. A self-deprecating smile lifted one corner of her mouth. That she was unable to dwell on her misery proved there were at least some advantages to life in the fast lane, after all.

WHEN THURSDAY ROLLED AROUND and she still hadn't heard from Eric, Janet was disconcerted to discover she missed him so much that she would have gone to his office wearing the infamous black corset and fishnet stockings just to see him again. Luckily, she didn't have to resort to anything nearly as dramatic. Since she had spent the day passing out samples of flavored almonds at a trade show in the Moscone Center instead of delivering balloons, she was wearing a favorite skirt and blouse. As it grew closer and closer to five o'clock, she paced back and forth in front of the booth, looking for her replacement. The second she spotted her, Janet hauled her back to the booth. The startled woman barely had time to remove her coat before Janet had thrust the tray of nuts in her hand and took off for Eric's office.

The elevator ride in Eric's building was just long enough to give her sweaty palms and a silly, anticipatory grin that she couldn't suppress despite several attempts to tell herself it was important that she look dignified. After identifying herself to the impossibly beautiful receptionist and being told she could go right in, Janet found herself suddenly feeling shy. She was halfway down the hall when Eric came out of his office to meet her. Considering the circumstances, she thought they handled the meeting extraordinarily well. Their greetings were impeccably polite and rigidly proper. As soon as the door clicked closed behind them, however, they were in each other's arms, their previous decorum lying in a rumpled pile at their feet.

"God, how I've missed you," he breathed into her hair, holding her close and lifting her off the ground in his enthusiasm.

"I was beginning to think the time we spent together in Sonoma was only another dream," she said. How wonderfully she fit into his arms; how right his arms felt around her.

"And have I convinced you differently?"

"I don't know—kiss me again so I'll be sure."

He complied with a deeply provocative kiss that left her reeling with want for him. His hands separated her coat and slipped up the silky material of her blouse to cup her breasts while his thumbs massaged her nipples until they were hard peaks. She tilted her head to the side, allowing him access to the sensitive hollow behind her ear. She was as helpless before the feelings that gripped her as an errant puff of cloud caught in the fury of a storm. "Please don't let go of me," she said, leaning heavily against him. "I don't think I could stand by myself."

"This is insanity," he murmured. "I want you so badly I can hardly breathe, and short of locking the doors and taking you over to the couch, there's not a damn thing I can do about it." He held the sides of her face and looked into her eyes. "How long—"

"I have to leave here by a quarter to six."

"That's fifteen minutes from now." With a heavy sigh of resignation, he put his arms back around her and held her as he would have held someone who was no more to him than a friend. "Janet . . . are you sure there's—"

"You can't possibly think I like this any more than you do." It hurt that he didn't recognize how hard she was trying to find time for them to be together.

"I don't." He led her over to the couch. "You'd think with all my training as a deadpan lawyer that I'd be able to handle missing you with a little more aplomb." Sitting on the forest-green watered-silk sofa, he pulled her down beside him and cradled her in his arms. "Detroit was pure hell. I spent so much time thinking about how having you there with me would have brightened that blighted city that I almost missed a couple of meetings."

"Believe me, you're not doing much for the quality of my studying, either. I had midterms this week, and for the first time ever, I'm actually worried about my grades."

How long would they go on like this before she would be willing to let him help her, he wondered, for what had to be the hundredth time. He felt so helpless. Here he was, a person who was paid an almost obscene salary for his power of persuasion, and he couldn't talk the most important person in his life into borrowing money from him. Knowing it was the wrong time and the wrong place, he still had to give it another try. "Janet . . . how much pressure would five hundred dollars a month take off of you?"

"A lot," she answered automatically and then suffered a sinking feeling when she realized where he was headed. "Eric, you're not going to start in on that loan thing again, are you?"

"What if I could get you another job with fewer hours but the same pay?"

She stiffened. "You mean some cushy thing where I file a few reports when I'm not filing my nails, my fantastic paycheck conveniently subsidized by you? Maybe you could even arrange a salary high enough for me to pay you back for the car insurance deductible, too," she added sarcastically.

"Why are you being so stubborn about taking my help?"

"Why are you being so insensitive?"

He decided it was time to try another line of reasoning. "You could think of me as your mentor. Lots of people, both men and women, have mentors."

"I believe, in this case, the correct term would be sugar daddy."

"I thought sugar daddy only applied if the man was old and doddering. I don't think I fit the bill on either account."

She twisted out of his arms, stood up and glared down at him. "There you go again, treating this as if it were some kind of joke."

He reached for her hand, but she pulled it away. "I'm sorry—I was only trying to keep us from getting into another fight."

"Well, guess what—you failed."

"Janet, we only have five minutes, please don't do this."

"How dare you put what's happening here today onto me." She knew exactly what she was doing, but she was powerless to control her actions. She had such a burgeoning feeling of hurt and frustration that she was striking out at the nearest person, and that person happened to be Eric. When he stood and tried to take her back into his arms she moved away, afraid that if she allowed herself even that much succor, she would break down. She knew she was walking perilously close to the edge as it was. The last thing she needed right then was to have his staff see her leave his office with eyes red and swollen from crying. She headed for the door. "I have to leave now," she said. "We'll talk about this later."

Eric watched her go out the door, and it was everything he could do to keep from going after her. He walked over to his desk and picked up the file on the Jacobson account. After blindly staring at it for several seconds, he uncharacteristically lashed out, throwing the file across the room. Papers littered the floor, looking obscenely out of place in the meticulously clean office.

"Dammit," he softly swore through clenched teeth. He could feel the only thing that truly mattered in his life slipping through his fingers, and he felt completely powerless. Several minutes passed, then his frown suddenly changed to a half smile. His step lighter than it had been in days, he went around the desk to find a telephone number he had put in the top drawer. By the time he finished his call, he was smiling again.

JANET MANAGED TO MAINTAIN her composure until she was inside the steel cocoon of her Volkswagen. Then, despite giving herself a stern lecture about the utter futility of crying, tears began to slither down her cheeks. She impatiently wiped them away and blinked to try to clear the new ones that immediately formed. But no matter how fast she blinked, her eyes seemed to fill faster. Finally she gave up and admitted she was crying.

Why was she being so stubborn, he had asked. Why, indeed? It wasn't that she doubted he loved her. She could see his love radiating from his eyes every time he looked at her. But there was something that kept her from accepting the help he wanted to give—something so powerful that it made her break out in a cold sweat simply thinking about it.

Even though everything about their short courtship had a slightly wacky tilt to it, she no longer harbored the smallest doubt that she loved him. *Then what was it?* Eric was handsome and charming and personable...not to mention rich enough to ensure they would never have the type of financial problems that had contributed to her and Robert's downfall.

There it was—that sick feeling in the pit of her stomach. It happened every time she thought about Eric's money. It wasn't just comfortable money, she reminded herself, it was money enough to buy anything that struck his fancy...including her. And what happened when someone with that kind of money grew tired of something they had? They simply tossed it out and bought something new.

The blood drained from her face. Did she subconsciously believe Eric considered her a disposable commodity? Her mind flashed back over their times together. He had been so quick to offer her his help . . . even going so far as to propose marriage. If he were someone who felt things deeply enough to make genuine long-range commitments, would he treat marriage as flippantly as he had?

Every ounce of reason she possessed told her she was being unfair. But it did nothing to change her feelings or lessen her fear. She now recognized her refusal to let him help her as a perverse subliminal attempt to keep him interested.

Pulling up to a red light, she dug through the glove compartment for a tissue and blew her nose. She tried to imagine what Eric would say if she were to explain her reasoning to him. She didn't have to imagine—her gut instinct told her. He would laugh.

ERIC STOOD on the corner of Market and Stockton, peering down Market, trying to pick out Janet's maroon-and-silver limousine through the swirling fog while nervously shifting a Neiman-Marcus bag from hand to hand. What, in his office, had seemed like a perfect solution to the problem they had discussed now didn't seem like such a hot idea. He tried to picture her reaction when she pulled up to the curb and realized he was her customer for the evening, but he was saved the mental exercise when the limousine swung around the corner and stopped in front of him. Before she could get out to open the door, he hopped in the passenger side.

"Eric . . . what are you doing?"

"If you recall, my car is still in the shop. I needed a ride."

Her eyes narrowed as she stared at him. "You were so desperate for transportation this evening that you offered a hundred-dollar bonus to get me as your driver?"

"He told you, huh?"

"In this business, a hundred-dollar bonus is big news. Everyone at the agency heard about it." With her face a mask that hid the cauldron of emotions bubbling inside, she returned her eyes to the road and engaged the turn signal. "Where to?" she asked, assuming her practiced professional attitude. She was determined to treat him like any other customer.

"Eventually, Fitzgerald's at the Park."

"Nice restaurant." She'd never been inside but had taken dozens of customers there and had heard every one of them rave about the meal and the service.

"I'm glad you think so."

"Why?"

"I had a hard time coming up with some place that was both quiet and elegant and still had food that was fairly uncomplicated. I thought it was about time I made up for that disastrous picnic I took you on."

"You expect me to go into a place like Fitzgerald's dressed like this?"

"I knew you would say that, so I had a friend help me pick this out for you." He laid the bag on the seat between them. "I promise you it's a lot closer to your size this time." He knew he was talking too fast, but he couldn't slow down. He felt he only had so much time and so many words to convince her.

"What is it?"

"A dress."

She felt as if she were trying to climb out of a pit that had sides made of sand. The more Eric tried to please her, the more she felt they were doomed. "And where am I to change into this dress?"

He refused to let the stony way she was responding to the evening he had planned discourage him. "Since the dinner reservations aren't until nine, there's plenty of time to make it to the Sea Cliff house first."

"I take it this means you've engaged my services for the entire evening?"

This time he couldn't ignore the chill in her tone and attitude. "What's wrong, Janet?" he said with a sigh.

When she answered, it was with wistful sadness. "You really have no idea, do you? How much is it going to cost you to be with me tonight?"

He thought for a moment. With the bonus he'd offered the agency, and if he were to add the price of the dress to everything else, it could conceivably reach a thousand dollars. "I'm not sure. I rarely pay attention to those kind of things."

"Let me make a guess, then. I'd say you'll be lucky to get away for less than three hundred." She left Powell and turned onto Lombard and headed west. They went several blocks in silence before she managed to speak again over the lump that had formed in her throat. "I know there are higher-priced hookers, but there aren't many."

His anger was instant. "That's a cheap shot—one I certainly don't deserve."

"Stop right there. It's my turn now." She was nearly yelling, she was so quick to defend her anger. "Were you or were you not planning to make love to me when we got to your house?"

Reluctantly he answered. "I admit I considered the possibility."

Damn! An unmistakable burning had started in the back of her eyes. "There may be kinder terms for what you had planned for me for this evening, but when all the flowery words are stripped away, it comes out exactly the same. When a man has to pay to sleep with a woman, that makes her a—"

"That's enough!"

His tone, the set of his jaw and the rigid way he held himself told Janet she had pushed him too far. He looked ready to explode.

"Pull over to the curb," he demanded, his fury barely in check.

They were still over a mile from his house, but she complied as soon as she found a space.

Without saying another word, he opened the door and got out. He started to walk away, turned and came back. Leaning down to talk to her through the window she had opened, he said, "If you ever get rid of that chip on your shoulder, call me. But don't make it too long; I won't wait forever." He turned and again walked away from her. Only this time he kept on walking.

As Janet watched him disappear into the dense fog, she made no attempt to stop the flow of tears or to control the sobs that wracked her shoulders. She knew she was watching the best thing that had ever happened to her walk out of her life, but she was helpless to stop him. A voice in the back of her mind kept repeating that she was lucky their relationship had gone no further than it had. Now she could cut her losses and get on with her life with only a fraction of the pain she would have felt had they become more deeply involved.

She listened to the voice, even though she knew it was lying to her. How much more involved could someone be than to give their heart? How much more pain was it possible to feel?

ERIC'S TOPCOAT flapped open as he walked along Lombard, but he was as oblivious to the frigidly damp air as he was to the people who stared at him as he passed. Where did someone begin picking up the pieces when his world had collapsed around him? For him, there was only one place, *The Promise*. He considered hailing a cab for the long trip home but couldn't face being with another person, so he just kept on walking. By the time he had walked down Lombard and through the Presidio, he figured he was halfway to *The Promise*, and since he was still unwilling to be around anyone, he continued his solitary journey. As though obsessed by one purpose, he crossed the Golden Gate Bridge, made his way through the steep hills of Sausalito and then down to the dock area. It was well past midnight when he was at last home.

Exhausted and chilled to the bone, he went straight to his bedroom, stripped off his clothes and collapsed on the bed, wrapping a huge down comforter around him as he turned his face to the wall. As he lay there, he became barely cognizant of the telephone ringing somewhere in the distance. Only wishing it would stop, he never once considered the possibility that it might be Janet who was trying to reach him through the call forwarding he had placed on the house phone.

JANET LET THE PHONE ring ten times before she gave up and went to bed. It was probably for the best that she hadn't been able to reach Eric. What would she have told him if she had? Somehow, after all they had been through that night, telling him she was calling just to

make sure he had made it home all right seemed un-
believably cruel. As long as she lived, she would never
forget the look on his face when she had accused him
of thinking of her as a hooker.

She went over to the closet where she had hung the
beautiful white dress she had found in the Neiman-
Marcus bag. It was made of a sensuous material that
would catch in a breeze and cling to her legs. It must
have taken Eric a long time to find such a dress in the
middle of winter. Was it possible she was wrong about
him? Were the problems between them created by her
own imagination? She knew the question would haunt
her for a long time to come.

10

JANET PURPOSELY OWNED an alarm clock that made an annoying buzz, because that was the only way she would get up in the morning. The trade-off was considerable—five to ten minutes of grumpiness as she fumbled around getting ready to start the day in return for a guarantee that she would get up. She was best left alone until she emerged from the shower, which usually gave her enough time to shed her irritation at being awakened by an obnoxious noise.

This morning, because the alarm had gone off at 3:00 A.M., barely two hours after she had gone to bed, her grumpiness was taking longer than usual to wear off. She ran her fingers through her hair and yawned as she made her way across the room to look out the window. It was dark outside—very dark. She cupped her hands around her eyes to try to see whether it was raining. There was moisture glistening on the metal swing set, but it was hard to tell whether it had come from the fog or was a remnant of yesterday's rain.

The mere thought of riding all the way to Livermore on the back of a motorcycle was enough to make her want to crawl back under the covers. With a concentrated effort, she resisted the impulse and headed for the bathroom, planning to stand under the hottest water she could tolerate. At least she could start the day warm.

Earthquake arrived promptly at three-thirty, looking as fresh and raring to go as he would in the middle of the day. Janet invited him into the house for a cup of coffee. After considering her invitation for a minute, he came inside. "We really should be leaving soon, though," he said, reaching up to take off his helmet. "We don't want to be late."

"God forbid," she groaned as she walked ahead of him into the kitchen. When she turned to hand him his cup, she almost dropped it. Since she'd seen him on Friday, he'd grown a full head of curly brown hair. "How did you do that?" she gasped, hardly recognizing him.

He grinned. "Easy. I took it out of a box this morning and glued it on. What do you think?"

Without the Mohawk he looked positively preppy. "I think your parents would get down on their knees and kiss the ground if they could see you."

"You think it will make them feel better about what I've done after I get arrested?"

"I wouldn't go that far." She handed him the cup. "Speaking of arrested, the leaders of this thing are aware that I'm not one of the volunteers, aren't they?" Protests had become so numerous and well organized since the seventy's, that most groups nowadays asked for volunteers to go to jail, rather than having the police haul everyone in. That worked out better for everyone. The police didn't have to search for places to hold hundreds of prisoners, and those going to jail could make plans ahead of time to be off work, or away from school, for a few days.

"Fear not. I made sure your name wasn't on the list."

She was having trouble keeping her eyes off him. The transformation from punk to preppy was amazing. She doubted anyone who had known him only with a Mohawk would be able to pick him out in a crowd, including herself. "Why the wig?" she asked, unable to contain herself any longer.

"I figured no one would take me seriously the other way," he said softly, radiating sincerity as poignantly as a lonesome puppy in a pet store window.

All thought of trying to talk him into letting her stay home so that she could go back to bed and get some sleep left her mind. If Earthquake cared so much about what they were doing that he was willing to compromise his normally militant attitude about his hair and dress, the least she could do was show up at the protest with him. "Come on," she said, taking his arm. "Isn't it about time we got going?"

By the time they arrived in Livermore, Janet was regretting every tender thought she had had in Palo Alto. She was convinced she was an idiot—no matter what the provocation—ever to have agreed to what had turned out to be a two-hour ride on the back of a motorcycle in weather colder than she had dared to imagine.

They passed the town and traveled east until they reached the Greenville Road exit, then turned off and went south for two and a quarter miles on a winding, narrow road. When Earthquake slowed down and made a right turn, she lifted her head from where she had had it sheltered in the middle of his back and looked around. They had pulled into an asphalted area that a sign identified as the East Gate. A guardhouse stood between locked chain-link-fence gates, and there was a sign demanding that they stop and display their badges. To the left were several brown buildings and a parking lot. Another sign, which said Visitor Center, pointed to the buildings. Everything behind the guardhouse was enclosed by a chain-link fence topped with three strands of barbed wire, which were angled outward to keep intruders from climbing over the top. Everywhere there were white placards that stated Tresspassing—Loitering Forbidden by Law. Less plentiful were the yellow placards evenly spaced along the fence. The printing on them was too small for her to read from that distance.

Other than the foreboding nature of the place, the most prominent feature was the lack of activity. "Where is everyone?" Janet asked, looking around the empty parking lot.

"I don't know," Earthquake replied, lowering the kickstand and reaching into his pants pocket for a piece of paper. He studied the paper for a minute before getting off the bike. "We're at the East Gate, right?"

She nodded.

"And today is Sunday?"

Again she nodded.

"Then I can't understand why we're the only ones here." He stuffed the paper back into his pocket.

"Maybe they all met someplace else and are planning to come in together. It would certainly make it look more impressive to do that than to have everyone drifting in singly." She didn't believe what she'd said, but Earthquake looked so crestfallen she felt she had to offer some thread of hope. She looked around again. "That must be what they're doing. I don't even see Casey's car anywhere." Casey had spent Saturday in Stockton visiting the parents of her latest boyfriend, which meant she would be coming from the opposite direction they had come.

"Oh, I must have forgotten to tell you, Casey's not going to be here today."

Janet let out an exasperated sigh. "Somehow that doesn't surprise me too much." Then another thought struck. "But if she's not coming, and you're going to jail, how am I supposed to get home?" There was no way she was going to manhandle his bike back over those mountains in the middle of Sunday traffic. Sitting on the back when the roads had been relatively clear had been bad enough.

"Don't worry, there's at least a dozen people coming from Stanford who would gladly give you a lift back home."

"If they ever get here, that is," she said glumly.

"Oh, ye of little faith."

There it was again, that indomitable cheerfulness. The way he was acting, a person would think the prospect of going to jail was the highlight of his life. She took his hand for balance and climbed off the bike, wondering how long it would take for the numbness to wear off from her buttocks and thighs. She stretched and then hugged herself against the cold. All in all, she decided as she looked around, what had started out as a miserable day was keeping itself directly on course. It was becoming painfully obvious that what she had hoped—to get to the lab, wave a sign for a few minutes and be on her way again—was not going to come to pass.

Earthquake started across the parking lot, and having nothing better to do, she followed. They stopped when they reached a place where there was a clear view of the buildings behind the fence. Lawrence Livermore Laboratory looked huge, but somehow it wasn't nearly as imposing as she had anticipated. The structures that were visible were mostly single story and had an air of impermanence about them, reminiscent of pictures she'd seen of military bases that had been hastily constructed during World War II. Maintenance trucks, stacks of tin drums and what looked like a conglomeration of spare parts made the area she could see clearly from where she was seem rather on the seedy side. She wasn't sure exactly what she had expected, but it certainly hadn't been this.

She looked around some more, noting how far the facility went back from the fence. She wasn't able to see to the other side. "This place is gigantic," she whispered, her voice filled with awe. She wasn't aware she had spoken her thoughts aloud until he answered.

"And dangerous."

She glanced up at the barbed wire, then over at the locked gate, subliminally taking in the profusion of warning signs against trespassing. Another chill slithered down her spine, only this one had nothing to do with the cold. If she hadn't been too crazy about coming here before, she was even less so now that she'd seen the facility. "What do you think we should do?"

"Huh?" Obviously as mesmerized as she was by all that surrounded them, Earthquake, too, had drifted into a world of his own.

"About being the only ones here," she prompted.

He shrugged. "I'm not about to let something like that stop me."

"You're not?" What better reason could there be?

"This is too important, Janet. We can't let one little setback stop us."

"We can't?" She was more than willing. But she could almost hear the wheels churning in his head, destroying her hopes for an easy getaway. "I don't know what's happened to everyone else, but we're here, and our voices count for something."

"Earthquake, you can't be serious." But she could see by the gleam in his eye that he was. "Be reasonable . . . what can only two people do?"

"History is filled with occasions when all it took was one person to make a difference."

"Name one."

"Joan of Arc."

"My God, Earthquake. If you recall, she was burned at the stake for her efforts. I'm not sure I'm ready for that kind of sacrifice."

"Okay, so Joan of Arc was a poor choice for an example. There have been plenty of others."

Realizing she would never be able to talk reason into him as long as they were still at the facility, she took his arm and tried to steer him over to the bike. "Why don't we go into Livermore," she said reasonably. "Surely there's a restaurant open by now where we could get some breakfast and talk this whole thing over."

"If we did that, by the time we got back here again it would be too late for us to do anything."

Precisely. "Better not to do anything at all rather than screw up what you do."

"Is that the best you can do?"

"It's still early."

"Ah, Jan, think of it. We might have a chance to change history today. Are you going to let that pass you by?"

"Would you please come down off that cloud you're perched on this morning? What makes you think whatever we do today is going to make any difference to anyone?"

"What makes you think it isn't?"

"I'm a realist."

"And I'm a dreamer, and I refuse to let my dream of a safe world for everyone be destroyed."

He said the words with such heart-wrenching sincerity, she could argue no more. "All right, Earthquake," she said with a resigned sigh. "What do you want me to do?"

"Help me get inside."

"*What?* Haven't you noticed all the signs telling you it's against the law to trespass in this place?"

"I'm not going to stay inside. I'm just going to hang the sign I brought with me on the side of that building and then come right back out again. As soon as I'm through, we can go home."

"What good is hanging a sign going to do? They'll just take it down as soon as they see it."

"If we're lucky, they won't see it before we get the media out here. Think, of it, Jan. Something like this could get picked up by the wire services and get national attention." He grasped her shoulders. "You know how people love 'little guy makes good' stories. This could start a grass roots movement that could snowball into—"

"Enough. If we're going to do this, let's get it done before people start showing up for work."

He gave her a bone-crushing hug. "Thanks, Jan. I'll never forget you for this."

As she watched him run back to the motorcycle for his sign, she shook her head in disbelief at how easily she had capitulated. Obviously her strong will and stubbornness only surged to the fore when it came to dealing with Eric. With anyone else, she was a pushover.

When Earthquake returned, he was wearing a smile that went ear to ear and was carrying a white sheet folded up under one arm. "You're never going to be able to get over that barbed wire without tearing yourself to pieces," she said in one last attempt to dissuade him.

"I have that all taken care of." He pulled a pair of wire snips out of his pocket.

"I see you came prepared." She should have known as much.

"Actually they're part of the tool kit I carry on the bike. I never thought they'd come in so handy."

Janet heard a car coming and turned to face the road. She breathed a sigh of relief when it kept going. "Could we please get this over with? I'm beginning to get the creeps."

"Where's your spirit of adventure?"

She glared at him.

"All right. I get the picture. Here—" he handed her the bedsheet "—you hold this while I climb over. When I'm on the other side, toss it to me." He stuck his toe in the fence and grabbed hold with both hands. When he was balanced near the top, he took the wire snips back out of his pocket and started to work on the barbed wire.

Janet noticed she was standing near one of the yellow signs and stepped closer to read it. On top was a notice that stated that the property they were trespassing on belonged to the United States Department of Energy. "Do you know who owns this place?" she asked, surprised by what she had discovered.

"Uh-huh . . . the Energy Department."

Score one for him. She stepped a little closer to read the fine print farther down. In legalese it told her the same thing the larger white signs proclaimed, only it took a hundred more words. The Department of Energy didn't want any unauthorized person on or about their property, and it was saying so in no uncertain terms. Because she was the type of person who read the backs of cereal boxes and the mastheads of magazines when there was nothing better available, she continued reading.

Whoever willfully violates the aforesaid regulation shall upon conviction thereof be punishable by a fine of not more than a thousand dollars.

A thousand dollars. "Earthquake—do you know what kind of fine is involved in this thing if we get caught?" She had grave doubts the courts would be as patient as Eric had been about getting paid.

"Uh-huh."

"And it doesn't bother you?"

"Ouch!"

"What happened?"

"I stuck a barb in my thumb."

"Are you all right?" she gasped.

"Don't get carried away, Jan. It's my thumb, not my throat."

She nervously shifted her weight to the other foot. "Are you about through?"

"Would you please calm down? I'm working as fast as I can."

She went back to reading the sign, skimming to the bottom, where she focused on the last line.

shall be guilty of a misdemeanor and upon conviction, shall be punishable by a fine not to exceed five thousand dollars or imprisonment for not more than one year.

"My God, Earthquake," she choked, her throat tightening convulsively. "Did you know what could happen to us if we're convicted?"

"Uh-huh," he answered in the same infuriating monotone.

"How can you be so calm about all of this?" she screeched.

"As I started to tell you earlier, if anything happens today, we'll be taken care of; so there's no real reason to get excited about it."

"Oh, yeah? And just who are these mysterious people who will be taking care of us—legal aid?"

"The group I belong to has lawyers—good lawyers—on retainer. They handle the cases for anyone who gets arrested during a protest. There's also a fund that pays the fines." His words were emphasized by the click of the wire cutter and the snap of the parting of the last strand of wire. As soon as he was sure the barbs weren't going to come back and snag him, he swung his leg over and hopped down to the other side. "Throw me the sheet."

Janet stood back and cocked her arm. Just as she was getting ready to let go, out of the corner of her eye she saw a movement. She glanced over to see what it was, and felt her heart sink to her toes. A parade of police cars was coming toward them.

Earthquake saw them at the same time she did. "Quick, toss me the sign. Maybe I still have time enough to get it up."

She gave him a look that said she thought he was a few cents short of a dime. "And just how are you planning to get in touch with the press to get this feat recorded?" She laid the sheet on the ground and prepared to raise her hands over her head, just in case she should be asked. "Please . . ." she begged him. "At this stage of the operation, I think it behooves us not to do anything that might make them mad."

Glancing behind her, she was stunned to see the entire parking lot full of police cars. As she watched, men in dark blue uniforms left their vehicles and started toward them, their hands resting ominously on their guns. She had a feeling her second scrape with the law was not going to go as easily as the first. She tried smiling. No one returned her smile. She let out a heavy sigh. It was going to be a long day.

A HALF HOUR after Janet had spotted the first police car, she and Earthquake were ensconced in its back seat, heading for a place called Santa Rita. Despite her repeated attempts to tell them she was not one of the people who were supposed to be arrested during the protest, they had handcuffed her and put her in the car.

"Don't worry, Jan," Earthquake said, sounding worried. "As soon as we get where we're going, I'll call the guy who's the head of our group. He'll get the lawyers down here right away, and they'll have us out before lunch."

"Uh-huh," she answered unenthusiastically. Since nothing else had gone according to plan today, why should the lawyers?

"Trust me. I know what I'm talking about on this."

They left the freeway and headed toward a group of white single-story buildings spread out over an area Janet guessed to be at least a hundred acres. A sign next to the road read: Alameda County Jail, Santa Rita. Behind the sign was another guardhouse and another chain-link fence. Only this time the barbed wire was angled to keep people in, not out. Behind the first fence was a second, this one topped with circles of concertina wire. She looked over at Earthquake and saw him pale. His eyes grew wide, and he tried to swallow. Finally he seemed to have realized just how much trouble they were in.

Because it was visiting day, there was a lot of confusion and a long line of cars outside the gate. The disruption spilled over into the area where Janet and Earthquake were taken for booking, allowing them to escape some of the normal routine long enough for Earthquake to make his phone call.

Somehow they had convinced the arresting officers that they were who they claimed to be and not part of some terrorist gang, and so they were being allowed more freedom than when they had first been taken into custody. While she waited for Earthquake, one of the men who had brought her in from the car had even offered her a cup of coffee, which she quickly and gratefully accepted. She was almost finished when Earthquake returned, looking more desolate than he had when he'd left.

"They won't help us," he said, his shoulders slumped in defeat.

"Why not?" she whispered, trying to keep the rising panic from her voice.

"It seems the protest that was supposed to take place today was postponed until next week because they had a promise from *Time* magazine that a reporter would be sent out to cover it. Anyway, now that we've been arrested, they feel they have to call the whole thing off or they'll wind up with egg on their faces. Needless to say, everyone is furious with me."

"And because of that one little mistake they're refusing to help us?"

"It's more than that. If they send anyone down to bail us out, it links them to what happened, and they feel that could hurt the organization."

Janet could already hear the prison doors clanging shut behind her and envisioned her stay as a long one. "So now what do we do?"

He tried smiling, but his lips only twitched in misery. "I don't suppose you happen to know any lawyers."

She sighed. "Only one." And she couldn't think of one reason why he would want to come to her aid again.

11

ERIC WENT AFTER the brass bell he was polishing with a vengeance, cleaning away dozens of years of neglect with forceful swipes of the polishing cloth. It was a project that didn't require skill or concentration, which was precisely the kind of mindless task he needed that morning because, no matter how hard he tried to prevent it, his thoughts invariably drifted back to Janet. The vibrant blue sky reminded him of her eyes; the breeze, of how her hair looked when it was ruffled by the wind. Even working on *The Promise* seemed less exciting than before since he was once again thinking of making his eventual odyssey on her alone.

He turned the bell over, and the clapper struck the side with a pure ringing tone, reminding him of the reason he had paid such a ridiculous price for the antique in the first place. He looked for pleasure in the memory, but it eluded him. Below deck he heard the telephone ring. Most of the calls that had come through in the past few days had been for Susan. Somehow word had gotten around town, erroneously, that she was back, and since he had put the San Francisco number on call forwarding, he had been inundated with people trying to get in touch with her. He considered ignoring the phone now.

Yet underneath the cool, unflappable facade of the corporate lawyer beat the heart of a dreamer; he couldn't give up hope that Janet would try to get in touch with him. Consequently, in spite of a voice that told him he was foolish to let his hopes build up, he headed down the stairs. By the time he reached the phone, it had rung seven times.

JANET SAID A SILENT PRAYER as she counted the number of times the phone rang. *Please be there, Eric. I really don't want to spend the night in jail.* She was about to replace the receiver when she heard his achingly familiar voice.

"Hello," he said, a little breathless from the hurried flight down the stairs.

"Eric, this is Janet."

He was at first too stunned to answer her. There was a broad chasm between dream and reality, and it took him a minute to make the journey. "To be honest, Janet, I didn't think you were going to call. But I'm glad you did."

She felt like a creep. She had known he would misinterpret why she'd phoned, but she hadn't imagined how happy he would sound or how badly she would feel. "I need your help, Eric . . ." she said. "Professionally."

He swallowed his disappointment; it hurt as it went down. "What can I do for you?" This time his voice was cool and dispassionate.

As succinctly as possible, she explained what had happened that morning. Eric asked several questions and told her he would be there as quickly as he could. He then asked her to give the phone to the desk sergeant so that he could ascertain whether the situation was something he could handle or if he needed to contact a criminal lawyer for assistance.

When Janet returned to where Earthquake waited, she was able to give him a reassuring smile. "He said not to worry. He's pretty sure he can get us out of here today."

Earthquake looked down at his feet. "I'll bet you'd like to forget we ever met."

How could she be mad at him when he was already so mad at himself? She put her arms around him and gave him a quick hug. "The only thing that could ever make me stop being your friend is if you gave up your dream of making this world a better place for me and my future children."

He gave her an embarrassed grin. "I'm not going to give up. I'm just going to go about things a little differently from now on."

"You have no idea how good that makes me feel."

"Do you suppose we'll be able to look back on this someday and laugh?" he asked, sounding highly skeptical of the possibility.

She knew he would never believe her if she told him how soon that day would come, so she simply smiled and led him over to the area where they had been told they could wait for their lawyer. They sat, hunched over on molded-plastic chairs, feeling like criminals and passionately hoping for a clean getaway.

ERIC ARRIVED two and a half hours later in a dilapidated pickup he had borrowed from one of the men at the boat yard. It took another hour for him to complete the paperwork for their release and another half hour after that to find Earthquake's motorcycle and load it into the truck.

Earthquake's presence acted as a buffer between Janet and Eric, allowing them to be polite and formally friendly to each other without their personal conflicts surfacing. On the way home, the road noise combined with fatigue worked its lethal magic on the vanquished protestors, and they soon fell asleep.

As the miles passed, Janet leaned more and more heavily against Eric. Her head rested on his shoulder, and her breathing was deep and regular. Seeing her again had stripped Eric of all pretense that he could give her up. They might have problems that seemed insurmountable, they might have personalities that seemed impossible to mesh and they might have an incredibly rocky road to travel before they would have a smooth ride—none of it mattered as much as the love that bound them. Now he only needed to convince her they were destined to be together. He had felt that Janet's getting in touch with him for his help might have been the first step in working things out between them. And then Earthquake had explained their predicament, and he had realized the phone call was nothing more than a last-ditch attempt to stay out of jail.

As they left the Sunol Valley, Eric looked down at her and noted the way the soft waves of her hair caressed her shoulders. A seed of warmth burst in his midsection when he thought of waking in the morning to see those raven curls resting on a pillow beside his own. Life would be so much simpler if he could drop Earthquake off at Stanford and just keep going. He could take Janet back to *The Promise* with him, set sail and stay at sea with her until they had worked out their problems. The idea seemed so inviting that he had a hard time convincing himself not to give it a try.

When they arrived at Stanford, Eric gently moved Janet so that she was leaning back against the seat, and then he helped Earthquake unload his motorcycle.

After receiving directions to Carol's house, he shook hands with Earthquake and told him again that he would be at the hearing and not to spend too much time worrying about the outcome.

Fifteen minutes later he pulled into Carol's driveway. "Janet . . ." He touched the side of her face in a lingering caress. Her only response was to softly groan and snuggle closer into his side. "Janet, you're home." This time he touched her arm.

Slowly she climbed out of the depths of sleep. What had happened earlier, where she was and who she was with came back to her with blinding clarity. With great reluctance she pulled away from Eric and sat up straight. After all that had transpired that day, to have just stayed where she was, pretending the two of them were friends again, would have been like floating on her own cloud from heaven.

She ran her hand through her hair and looked out the cracked windshield at the front of the house. Her gaze dropped to her hands, then to the worn-out floor mat on the passenger side of the seat. She could look anywhere but at him. "I want you to know how much I appreciate the fact that you gave up your Sunday to bail me out of another jam."

"Coming to your rescue was a lot more interesting than what I was doing."

Wonderful—she had become an amusing diversion. "Well, I'm sure you'd like to get back to whatever it was you were doing, so I'll let you go now." She started to scoot over to open the door, but Eric reached out and caught her arm.

"I'm not in any hurry, if you'd like to sit here and talk awhile."

She hesitated. "There is one thing.... I don't know what to do with the dress you bought for me." It was the only way she could think of to begin a discussion of what had happened between them last Thursday. What she hoped he would say was that he wanted her to keep the dress and to perhaps even wear it for him that night. Surely he would realize she had the rest of the day free.

But her question did not at all elicit the response she wanted. Eric only heard that she wanted to dispose of something he had given her and that brought back all the pain and anger he had felt in the limousine. "I don't care what you do with it," he said evenly, his hands tightening around the steering wheel until the knuckles grew white. "Give it away or throw it away. It's all the same to me."

She covered her hurt by responding to his anger with haughty dismissal. "How could I have forgotten so quickly just how indifferent you are to money?"

"It's not that I'm indifferent, it's that you're paranoid about it. Money, or the lack of it, doesn't control my life the way it does yours."

"Easy for you to say. What could you possibly know about the lack of anything?"

How could he be sitting here fighting with her when what he really wanted to do was take her in his arms and hold her and make love to her until all that separated them became as insignificant as single grains of sand on a beach. "This is getting us nowhere," he said.

"You're right." Her hand went to the door handle. "Here you've been a real friend and gone way out of your way to help me out today, and my way of thanking you is to behave like a bear with a thorn in its paw." She climbed out of the truck. Before she closed the door she forced herself to look at him, seeking one last glimpse to carry with her. "I want you to know I haven't forgotten that I still owe you for the deductible on the car."

Eric heaved a weary sigh. Would she never understand that money stood between them only because it was important to her? "Forget it. It doesn't matter anymore."

Oh, but it did matter, she ached to tell him. Now that they were no longer struggling to see each other, the debt was their only link. She would hang on to that link until every dime was paid back. "I can't forget it," she said softly.

"Then send the money to your favorite charity. I don't want it." Every payment would remind him of what he had lost and open old wounds like a knife. "I have to go now, Janet. I promised the man I borrowed the truck from that I would have it back before five o'clock." He had to get away from her before he did something foolish like grabbing her and making her come with him to some remote spot where there would only be the two of them and they would have no choice but to talk to each other.

"Oh—I'm sorry. I didn't know." She stepped away from the cab and closed the door. As she watched him back out of the driveway her hand started to come up from her side to wave goodbye, but she stopped the motion by hugging herself. It was a lonely, forlorn motion that accentuated her feeling of isolation. She turned to walk up to the front porch. The door opened before she had reached for the knob.

"Who was that man?" Carol asked, not even trying to disguise the fact that she had been watching them through the window.

"Eric."

"That was Eric Stewart? He's the one you're letting drift away?"

"*Letting?*" As if she had any choice in the matter.

"Yes, letting," Carol said with a frustrated sigh. "How hard have you tried to patch things up between you?"

"Carol, there are some things a patch just won't cover." She hung her jacket up in the hall closet. "I'm going to bed. If anyone calls, tell them I'm not here."

"Wait a minute," she said with reluctant acceptance of Janet's decision in her voice. "You didn't say how the protest went."

She closed her eyes and shook her head. "I'll tell you about it later. Right now I want to forget today ever happened." She turned down the hall and went into her bedroom, convinced all she had to do was lay her head on the pillow, and blessed, forgetful sleep would automatically come to her.

A half hour later, unable to get thoughts of Eric out of her mind even after counting 1,832 sheep, she got up and went over to the closet to get her bathrobe, planning to go to the kitchen and indulge herself with a glass of milk and cookies. As soon as she opened the door, her eyes went to the elegant white dress Eric had bought for her. Without conscious thought, she reached out to touch the silklike material. Letting her fingers absorb the sensuous feel of the fabric, she slid them across the plunging bodice. It was the most beautiful dress she had ever seen: cut to accentuate her best features, classic and yet stylish...and it was her size. How long had it taken Eric to select the dress for her? Who was the friend he had said helped him? Questions she would never ask, answers forever a mystery.

She couldn't give the dress away, and yet she couldn't keep it. To go to her closet every day and face such a powerful reminder of what had almost been hers was nothing short of masochistic. As soon as she had a free Sunday, she would return the dress to Neiman-Marcus and give the money to Eric. He wouldn't like it, but at least her conscience would be clear.

ON MONDAY Janet received the results of her midterms. They weren't as good as previous midterms, but neither were they as bad as she had feared. She was amazed to discover her world hadn't collapsed at her first B-minus and that she wasn't in a panic to bring it up by the final.

Tuesday, she spent the day delivering balloons to make up for missing her turn as a clown the previous Thursday. She slipped into a blue funk after making her last delivery to the children's cancer ward at San Francisco General Hospital. By the time she returned to the Anything Goes Agency, she was so depressed that when she washed off her clown makeup, she didn't bother putting her normal street makeup on afterward.

Michael Stephens, the co-owner of Coachman's, was waiting for her when she arrived for her evening shift. "Just two fares tonight, Janet. A quick run to take some rock star to the airport, then a night on the town for some guy and his girlfriend."

"Thanks, Mike. I can use the study time."

"How were the midterms?"

"Nothing to write home about."

He accompanied her to the limousine and stood by the time clock to talk to her while she went through her normal routine of checking out the car she would use that night. "You don't look so good tonight. Is there something wrong?"

"I'm just a little tired." And a little blue and a little heartbroken.

"Well, for God's sake, don't let yourself get run-down. I don't want you getting sick on me. I can't afford to have you out; you're the best driver I've got."

"That's nice to hear." She looked up from checking the front tire. "Does that mean you're thinking about giving me a raise?"

"You're already making more than any of the other drivers who work here."

"That sounds really impressive, Mike, but you and I know ten cents an hour above scale isn't exactly—"

"Oh, darn!" Mike comically exclaimed when the office phone rang and interrupted her. "Gotta go, Janet. We'll be sure to talk about this some other time."

She smiled. Their ten-cents-an-hour thing was an ongoing joke. Something, whether it was the phone or a customer or a suddenly remembered appointment, always prevented them from finishing.

As soon as she was through with the car, Janet went into the back room and changed into her uniform. A few minutes later she was on her way over to the Saint Francis Hotel to pick up her first ride.

She got a kick out of transporting celebrities and had learned to judge their personalities from the way they behaved during their rides. Those who were still new to the limelight were generally either brash and obnoxious in their efforts to appear accustomed to luxury, or they were pointedly unimpressed. Those who had been in the business longer usually fit into the basically-good-folks-who-happened-to-make-it-big category or were prigs who would have been a pain in the neck no matter what field they had chosen to make their living in.

Tonight her ride was a young woman dressed in black leather pants and a white pirate's shirt. Her waist-length hair was striped black and white. Her very straight-looking companion was a woman in her mid-forties with an easy smile and a hearty laugh. The young woman was refreshingly in awe of everything that was happening to her. On their way to the airport, she insisted that Janet keep the glass panel between them open so they could talk.

After she had asked Janet a dozen questions about what it was like being a chauffeur in San Francisco, she eagerly answered some of Janet's questions. She told her she knew being a rock star was a transitory thing and that the entertainers who managed any kind of longevity in the field were few and far between. Consequently, she intended to touch and feel and see everything she could while she was still on top and carry the memories with her when she moved on to something else.

Their time together did so much to improve Janet's mood that she turned on the radio and found herself singing country and western music along with Kenny Rogers and Dolly Parton as she returned to the city. She made it to the Sloat Boulevard address, where she was to pick up her next customer, ten minutes early, so she parked down the block and watched an old woman sitting on a bench feeding a lone gray pigeon.

When the ten minutes had passed, she pulled up in front of the apartment building, got out of the car and opened the iron gate that led to a courtyard and the apartments. She glanced at the lower-level numbers and realized the number she wanted was on the second floor.

When she knocked, a stunning, statuesquely built woman with red hair answered. Unlike most people with red hair and easily sunburned skin, this woman's complexion was tanned to a golden bronze and was clear of freckles. Her eyes were a deep, sultry brown, the kind Janet's father called bedroom eyes. She was dressed in a slinky black jumpsuit that had long sleeves and no back. Her full breasts, obviously unencumbered by anything as basic as a bra, moved freely when she turned to accept her coat from ... *My God*, Janet mentally screamed. It was *Eric*!

Janet's eyes flew open as she unintentionally registered intense shock at seeing him there. They then narrowed again as shock turned to fury. How dare he do something like this to her? Who did he think he was, hiring her to drive him around with another woman after all they had meant to each other? She glared at him and was gratified to see he at least had the courtesy to look embarrassed.

The woman turned to Eric and lightly, intimately touched his arm. "I have to get my bag," she said, her voice every bit as sultry as her eyes. "I'll be right back." She made it sound like a promise fraught with possibilities.

When she had gone, Eric stepped closer and spoke to Janet in a hushed voice. "I'm really sorry about this." He nervously reached up to rub the back of his neck. "I specifically asked the agency to send a man to avoid any possibility that we might run into each other. I'd certainly understand if you didn't want to drive for me tonight, and if you want me to, I'll call for another limousine."

"Hey, no problem." She refused to let him see how upset she was. "As far as I'm concerned, you're just another fare."

"I'm happy to hear you feel that way. It'll make the evening a lot easier on both of us."

If she were just a little taller and weighed maybe forty or fifty pounds more, she would have gladly choked him. "It seems silly for us not to be friends, right?"

"Absolutely."

The redhead came back, possessively taking his arm and lovingly gazing up at him with her adoring, doe-like eyes. "I'm ready, Eric," she breathed.

Ready, willing and, if Janet was any judge of such things, quite able. Inside, she seethed, her anger barely under control. Outside, she maintained her composure and managed to give Eric her most dazzling smile. "And where will you and the lady be going this evening, Mr. Stewart?" she said through clenched teeth.

"The lady's name is Rachel Hopkins, Ms Franklin."

Nodding her head to the woman, Janet said, "Ms Hopkins."

"Oh, please—make it *Miss* Hopkins." Rachel gave Eric another lingering look. "None of this feminist stuff for me," she cooed. "Deep down I'm just an old-fashioned girl."

Janet thought she was going to be sick.

"As for where we're going . . ." Eric said, meeting Rachel's gaze with one Janet considered equally insipid. "We thought we'd start at Fitzgerald's at the Park and then go to the Top of the Mark for drinks and dancing."

She wouldn't have to be any taller, only about twenty-five pounds heavier, and she'd gleefully stomp on his perfectly polished black leather shoes. How dare he take this woman to the restaurant he had picked out for her! "Well, we certainly don't want to get you there late, now do we?" She motioned them forward with a wave of her hand.

The drive across town was excruciatingly long. She seemed to hit every red light and could have sworn she got stuck behind every rubbernecking tourist in the city. The delay forced her to listen to a constant barrage of high-pitched laughter through the glass partition. Since Eric hadn't shown any particular prowess in the humor department when she'd been with him, she assumed he'd either been saving it all for tonight, or the redhead was one of those women who thought her laugh was sexy.

Finally they arrived at the restaurant. Janet pulled up to the entrance to let them off, found a parking place and came back to inform the doorman where she was parked so he could summon her when Eric was ready to leave. When she got back to the car, she didn't even bother pulling her books out from under the seat. She knew any attempt to read them would be an exercise in futility. What hurt the most was the seeming ease and incredible speed with which Eric had apparently got over her. Here she was, struggling to make it through each day, unable to sleep because of a white dress hanging in her closet, and he was going out on the town. *And she was driving him!*

Oh, please . . . make it Miss *Hopkins,* her mind mimicked. *I'm just an old-fashioned girl.* Janet just bet Rachel Hopkins was old-fashioned. She was the kind who wouldn't think twice about accepting money from Eric, and for far less reason. What was he doing with someone like her? She wasn't his type at all. He needed someone who was his equal, not a simpering wimp. Dammit, what he needed was someone like her.

The two hours it took them to have dinner seemed like twenty. By the time Janet had got around to wondering how many evenings like this one it would take to produce an ulcer in her churning stomach, Eric had opened the door and climbed in the front seat beside her.

"The doorman was busy, so I came to tell you we're ready to leave now. Rachel's waiting for us at the restaurant."

Janet was sorely tempted to drive off and forget the waiting Rachel. "Yes, sir." She started the car, and as was her custom on cold nights, let it warm awhile.

"I can't tell you how much it means to me to have you accept this evening the way you have, Janet. I was afraid we wouldn't be able to be friends, but I can see I was wrong. From now on I'll have no hesitation about asking for you to be my driver when I go out."

Before she could think her answer through, the words were out. "Eric, I don't think this Rachel person is right for you." She saw a muscle twitch on the side of his cheek and waited for the explosion.

"I appreciate your concern, but I'm sure you'll understand if I question your ability to judge who is right or wrong for me. Obviously both of us struck out in that department once already."

"I only meant—"

"That she's nothing like you?" he said softly.

His words had been spoken in a way that prevented her from telling what feelings lay behind them. Was it sarcasm or anger, mockery or a gentle plea? She would have preferred the latter, but the piercing look he gave her made her feel it was more likely one of the others.

"That's not what I meant." But it was precisely what she had meant.

"Tell me, then, what kind of woman would you choose for me?"

If she answered, she would surely give herself away. "I'm sorry I brought it up." She switched her attention to the car, putting it in gear and pulling into traffic. "Who you do or don't go out with is none of my business."

"On the contrary. I expect my friends to take an interest in what I do. I'm disappointed if they don't."

"Well, I'm afraid this particular friend is going to have to pass on giving you advice on your love life." She almost choked on the words.

"I'm disappointed in you Janet. I was counting on more."

She pulled up to the front of the restaurant. His statement, the way he said it, baffled her. Counting on more? Just what had he meant by that? Before she had a chance to ask him, he was out of the car and opening the door for Rachel.

The rest of the evening consisted of taking Eric and Rachel to the Top of the Mark for drinks and dancing, waiting around for a frustrating three hours, then driving them back to Rachel's apartment. When Janet got out of the car to open the door for them, Eric looked at Rachel with passion-filled eyes and told Janet it would be a little while before he returned.

Janet seethed for the first fifteen minutes. The next fifteen minutes she boiled. The half hour after that, she was in a rage. Of all the thoughtless, heartless things Eric had done to her that evening, this one easily took the prize. How could he leave her waiting outside while he wooed that . . . that . . . vapid creature?

Well, she wasn't going to wait any longer. She was going up to Miss Hopkins's apartment and give Eric Stewart a piece of her mind. After which, he could call a cab—or walk all the way home, for all she cared. She'd be damned if she'd drive him around the block.

12

JANET GOT OUT of the car, slamming the door behind her with a vengeance. She stomped up to the iron gate and went into the courtyard, which she found eerily dark. Hadn't these people heard that thieves did their best work in dimly lit places?

Feeling her way along the rough stucco wall by only the ghostly light of a mist-covered full moon, she found the stairs. She wrapped her hand around the icy railing and started to climb. She was at the first landing when a feeling of apprehension struck. As she stood there trying to comprehend the feeling, the back of her neck began to tingle. Something—a sixth sense, invisible vibrations, whatever—told her she wasn't alone. Her heart racing, she tried to see into the deep shadows near the top of the stairs. Her breath caught in her throat when she made out the form of a man. He was hunched over in a crouching position, poised as if ready to spring.

She froze. Her heart slammed against her chest. Not knowing what to do, she did nothing. Suddenly the man moved toward her. She let out a piercing scream.

"For God's sake, what's the matter with you?"

Her hand over her speeding heart, she blinked, again trying to erase the darkness. "Eric?" she gasped, positive she had recognized his voice.

"Janet?"

"What are you doing sitting out here on the stairs in the dark?" she demanded, her intense relief producing a flash of anger. "You nearly scared me to death."

A door opened behind him, then another somewhere close by. "What's going on out there?" a deep male voice demanded.

"It's all right," Janet quickly answered. That's all they needed—someone charging down the stairs on a rescue mission. "I just ran into something in the dark, and it frightened me."

She heard a muted grumbling and then the word, "Women," spoken as if that explained everything. The sound of a pair of doors closing followed the grumbling.

She turned her attention back to Eric. "Now would you please tell me why you're lurking around out here?"

"I'm not lurking, I'm sitting."

"Dammit, Eric, give me a straight answer, or I'm going to scream again. Only this time, I'll make it loud enough to bring the house down. And when someone asks me what's wrong, I'll tell them you tried to assault me."

"All right, you win," he said with a resigned sigh. "I wanted you to think I was inside with Rachel."

Stunned by his confession, she leaned against the railing and thought for a minute. At last the evening made sense. Eric had carefully planned everything that had gone on in an effort to make her jealous. And although she knew he wasn't aware of it yet, his plan had succeeded beyond what was probably his wildest dream.

She climbed the few steps that separated them and sat down. She could see him clearly now. He had turned his collar up and had his arms folded tightly across his chest in an effort to ward off the cold. "I don't understand why Rachel made you wait out here?"

"She thinks I left a long time ago. She had an early flight tomorrow, and I didn't want to keep her up any longer than I already had."

Janet reached for his hand. It felt like a chunk of ice. "Just who is this Rachel?"

"A friend of Susan's."

"And a consummate actress."

Several seconds passed in meaningful silence. "Janet, we can't go on like this."

"I know," she said softly, expressing a world of meaning in the two words.

Her answer caught him off guard. He had anticipated more of a fight or, at least, a little more resistance. His success made him push harder. "I want you to come home with me tonight so we can get everything that's keeping us apart out in the open and settle it once and for all."

"All right."

"All right?" he almost shouted. "You're going to capitulate that easily, after I've been out here all this time freezing my. . ." He struggled for a suitable word. The ones that came to mind belonged in a locker room. "What I've been freezing off is beside the point." He raked his hand through his hair. "If you figured out what I was doing, why didn't you say something earlier?"

"You're giving me more credit than I deserve. The only thing I figured out during those miserable hours you forced me to wait for you is that I love you beyond reason...beyond stubbornness, too." Her voice dropped to a whisper. "I've decided that if at all possible, I would much rather live my life with you than without you."

He no longer felt the cold as the warmth of her words penetrated him, creating a joyous swell of pleasure. He cradled her face in his hands. "I love you," he said. She came forward to receive his kiss. The touch of his lips erased the pain of their separation. The trauma of the past week had created a compelling, nearly compulsive desire to be in the loving shelter of his embrace, to feel the healing touch of his love. Her arms wrapped around his neck. "Didn't you say something about taking me somewhere?" she murmured against his lips as relief gave ground to passion.

Reluctantly he held her away from him. He wanted more than tonight from her. He wanted her with him the rest of his life. "I have to warn you, Janet," he said, his voice deadly serious. "Once I get you on board *The Promise*, you're not getting off again until we've decided once and for all how we're going to start seeing each other on a regular basis."

She ignored his warning. There was no longer any doubt in her mind that they would find a way to be together. "On board?" she repeated, confused. Could all Eric's vague references to promising things have been about a boat called *The Promise*?

Was it possible he had never told her where he really lived? "I thought you knew my home was in Sausalito."

"I did. But you never mentioned your home was a boat." How could she not know something like that about him?

"It's where I've lived for the past five years."

She took his hand and stood up. The information that Eric lived on a boat didn't come close to fitting in with the mental image she had created of the strait-laced, rich corporate lawyer. Obviously there were some important things she didn't know about Eric that it was high time she did. "I want to see this boat."

Eric got up more slowly than she had, testing his stiff legs before standing on them. "I take it this enthusiasm to accompany me means you've agreed to my terms?"

She hesitated before answering, an impish twinkle in her eyes. "What are my options?"

"You don't have any."

"Then I agree."

"A most wise decision on your part," he said with a sinister quality in his tone. "Had you not agreed, I was prepared to kidnap you and, if necessary, carry you off in the classic Rhett Butler manner. And the way my legs feel right now, I'm not sure we would have made it very far."

"You mean you would have taken me against my will?" She tried to sound aghast.

He took her into his arms and gave her a kiss filled with exquisite promise. She responded like a banked fire to dry kindling. "Would it have been against your will?" he breathed, as shaken by the electricity that passed between them as she was.

"No," she admitted, leaning into him, fervently wishing they were somewhere private so they could pursue what they had so unthinkingly started in the middle of a freezing staircase. Suddenly the electricity came back on, bathing them in blinding light.

"It's time for us to get out of here," he said, taking her hand and heading out to the car.

Although it was against company policy, Janet asked Eric to drive. She didn't want to think or concentrate on anything but him. She snuggled into his side. A wondrous sense of contentment made the fog-shrouded world they passed through appear more beautiful than ever before.

In what seemed only a short time, they were entering the municipal parking lot along the front of the pier in Sausalito. Janet had brought countless customers to this artist's colony, but she had never come back on her own to explore the quaint, expensive shops or to eat in any of the restaurants that afforded a spectacular view of San Francisco across the bay.

It was well-known that to live and play in Sausalito required money—lots of it. The yachts she could see from the parking area were easily in the million-dollar range. Even before she had got out of the car, she was feeling intimidated by the flagrant wealth that surrounded them. She chided herself for the feeling, but it refused to go away. She fought to catch her breath past the heaviness in her chest and forced a smile when Eric came around to take her hand and lead her onto the pier.

Because she had worked several yacht shows for the Anything Goes Agency, she was aware of the staggering cost of even the small ships they passed. Many of the larger ones were bigger than her parent's home in Portland. And it wasn't only the purchase price of the yachts that impressed her; it was the ongoing cost of the large crews required to run them and the people needed to keep them clean—not to mention that it would probably take a large chunk of her annual salary just to tie up a boat at this pier. She couldn't shake the insidious feeling that she didn't belong in a place like this and would never be able to fit in with people who lived this kind of life. She had nothing in common with them.

As they neared the end of the pier, her gaze swept past all the opulence and focused on a decrepit-looking sailboat that looked as if it had spent the majority of its life beneath the sea rather than on top of it. She couldn't imagine what that poor relation was doing hobnobbing with all its rich cousins, but she liked its plucky attitude.

Eric opened a waist-high gate leading to the stairs that would take them to the lower level where the boats were actually secured. They continued to walk until there was only one vessel—a sleek ninety-six-foot Broward Motor Yacht—between them and the sailboat. Without thinking, Janet headed in the direction of the Broward.

"Where are you going?" Eric asked, grabbing her arm.

She searched his face. "This isn't your boat?" she said, pointing to the Broward.

"A *motorboat*?" He spit the word out as if it had put a bad taste in his mouth.

"You mean . . ." she gasped, her gaze flying to the sailboat, "*that's* yours?" It looked even worse close up.

Eric looked at *The Promise* and tried to see it through her eyes. He guessed it might look pretty bad to anyone who knew nothing about quality sailing vessels, especially when compared to its pristine fiberglass neighbors. Still, her undisguised shock rankled. "Are you disappointed?" he asked, trying to hide his own sense of letdown.

She glanced at the boat, then back at him. "Are you kidding?" she squealed, throwing her arms around him. "I'm ecstatic. Any man who would spend his time restoring a boat like this could never throw something away just because it had been around awhile."

He didn't understand, but he didn't care. It felt too good to hear the happiness in her voice. "I imagine someday you're going to explain what you mean by that."

"It isn't important." She stood on her toes and gave him a kiss. "Oh, Eric, why didn't you bring me here a long time ago?"

"If you recall, there was a small problem about finding the time to take you anywhere." He didn't need to know what had caused the transformation in her. All that mattered was that she seemed to have finally accepted who and what he was. He bent and picked her up in his arms. Slowly he turned in a circle, returning the kiss she gave him, feeling a liquid fire race through his veins. If happiness could be bottled and saved for future hard times, he was convinced this moment would provide a life's supply.

He carried her on board *The Promise* and didn't put her down until they had reached the stairs to go below. He asked her to wait while he went ahead to turn on the lights. He felt anxious to see her expression when she saw what he hoped would someday be her home.

As soon as Janet saw the lights go on, she followed him below. But she stopped before reaching the last step, overwhelmed by the warmth and beauty of the room she saw—in such stunning contrast to the outside of the ship. Everywhere there was the glow of natural wood, lovingly and painstakingly restored. The furniture had been carefully selected to give a feeling of welcome and was covered in muted earth tones. Touches of yellows and rusts added color, and vibrant green plants growing in the corners and on tables added warmth. On the far wall was a fireplace with a marble mantle.

"It's beautiful, Eric," she said simply, at a loss for words to express her complex feelings. She went over to stand beside him, putting her arm around his waist and leaning her cheek against his chest. "I've been so unfair to you. Instead of seeing you as you really are, I let my prejudices against rich people get in the way. I misjudged you entirely."

"Does this mean you've decided to let me help you with school?" He knew the timing wasn't the best, but he so desperately wanted things settled between them that he took a chance.

She stiffened. It would be hard to let go of the complete control she had gained over her own life. "As long as we both know it's only a loan."

"One that will be canceled the day we get married."

She tilted her head back to look at him. "How would you know I wasn't marrying you just to pay off a debt?"

Her screwy logic made him smile. "Janet, if I have to fight this hard to get you to take money from me in the first place, how could I ever think you'd marry me to get out of paying it back?" He bent to kiss her upturned mouth. "But if feeling indebted to me would get you to the altar any faster, I'd gladly turn all my assets over to you first thing in the morning."

She returned his kiss, parting her lips in an open invitation for him to deepen what he had started. "Oh, Eric . . ." she sighed, leaning against him, her legs suddenly feeling wobbly. "There isn't an ounce of fight left in me—every corner's filled with loving you."

How many men who dared to dream such uncompromising dreams had seen them come true? He had waited for a woman like Janet far longer than what had seemed a reasonable time, yet he had never given up hope that he would find her. And she was everything—no, she was more—than he had dreamed she would be. He lowered his mouth to hers. "Tell me again."

She would tell him. Tomorrow and the next day and all the days in all the years they would have together. But right now it was time to show him. She put her arms around his neck and brought him to her, giving him a kiss that left no doubt about her intentions.

"I like your style, lady," he murmured, sweeping her into his arms. He picked her up and carried her into the bedroom in the best Rhett Butler tradition. Only, unlike Scarlet, Janet never thought to protest.

Harlequin Temptation

COMING NEXT MONTH

Can you keep a secret?

You can keep this one plus 4 free novels

Harlequin Intrigue

Because romance can be quite an adventure.

What readers say about Harlequin romance fiction...

"I absolutely adore Harlequin romances! They are fun and relaxing to read, and each book provides a wonderful escape."
—N.E.* Pacific Palisades, California

"Harlequin is the best in romantic reading."
—K.G.* Philadelphia, Pennsylvania

"Harlequins have been my passport to the world. I have been many places without ever leaving my doorstep."
—P.Z..* Belvedere, Illinois

"My praise for the warmth and adventure your books bring into my life."
—D.F.*Hicksville, New York

"A pleasant way to relax after a busy day."
—P.W..* Rector, Arkansas

*Names available on request.

WORLDWIDE LIBRARY IS YOUR TICKET TO ROMANCE, ADVENTURE AND EXCITEMENT

Experience it all in these big, bold Bestsellers— Yours exclusively from WORLDWIDE LIBRARY WHILE QUANTITIES LAST